What was Matt Long doing here long years after he'd left?

Jenny had hoped to never see him again.

When he stepped out of the truck, still as gorgeous as ever, Jenny's traitorous heart twitched, but she forced it to settle down. Fast. Shallow charm and a killer grin wouldn't turn her head this time around. She'd learned her lesson when he'd run out on her.

He could no longer set her skin on fire. The only heat that burned within her for him now was anger.

"You have a lot of nerve coming back to Ordinary," she said. "Especially after the way you left. You couldn't have said goodbye? Or left a note?"

He stopped when he saw her. His mouth dropped open then just as quickly closed. The line of his jaw became hard. Then he shrugged.

No conscience.

Good to know. She felt better about the decisions she'd made. She'd been right to do what she'd done, and to hell with Matt's feelings. They weren't her concern.

Dear Reader,

Sometimes the best things in life are the surprises.

Just when we think we have everything figured out, and know exactly where we want our lives to go, surprises send us for a loop, raise their figurative heads and say, "You might want to rethink where you're headed."

Matthew Long first appeared in *No Ordinary Cowboy* as a love 'em and leave 'em cowboy, but *I* wasn't ready to love him and leave him. I knew he had a whole lot more going on than he let the world see.

Matt believes he would make a terrible father, but once he sees Jesse for the first time and realizes that Jesse is his son, his life changes irrevocably.

The question then is whether Matt is up to the challenge, but we romance readers expect a lot from our heroes and our heroes hate to disappoint us.

Sometimes the things we most fear, brought on by those uncontrollable surprises in life, stand up and shout, "Sure your life was okay the way you planned it, but you're going to love this even more!"

Enjoy Matt's story!

Mary Sullivan

This Cowboy's Son
Mary Sullivan

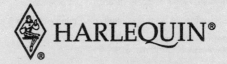

HARLEQUIN®

TORONTO • NEW YORK • LONDON
AMSTERDAM • PARIS • SYDNEY • HAMBURG
STOCKHOLM • ATHENS • TOKYO • MILAN • MADRID
PRAGUE • WARSAW • BUDAPEST • AUCKLAND

Recycling programs
for this product may
not exist in your area.

ISBN-13: 978-0-373-71653-1

THIS COWBOY'S SON

www.eHarlequin.com

Printed in U.S.A.

ABOUT THE AUTHOR

Mary Sullivan loves writing about children. That's why you'll find them in many of her stories. She loves to watch how they affect us in real life and then writes about how they affect her heroes and heroines. If we allow them to, children can challenge us as parents and caregivers and extended family members and in society as a whole to be the best that we can be. Readers can reach her through her Web site at www.MarySullivanbooks.com.

Books by Mary Sullivan

HARLEQUIN SUPERROMANCE
1570—NO ORDINARY COWBOY
1631—A COWBOY'S PLAN

CHAPTER ONE

WIND WHIPPED through the valley and howled around the old house like a widow keening.

A crack of thunder shook the earth. Rain pelted the windshield faster than the wipers could clear it away, blurring the outline of the cabin.

Matthew Long swore he could hear years-dead voices whispering things better left unsaid. Grief clung to this place like a bad dream, still breathed his father's obscenities and his mother's lunatic ravings.

He wished that Jenny Sterling could have found somewhere else to ride out this storm other than the house he'd grown up in.

Lightning flashed the midnight sky with midday brightness, exposing a still life of the land on which Matt had hoped to never again step foot. Weeds had obliterated any trace of the small garden his mother had once planted in the yard. A hole the size of a pebble marred one of the living room's windows.

The flat roof of the veranda listed like a drunken sailor.

The house looked forgotten and lonesome.

Warm light flickered in the cabin's windows and wood smoke scented the air. Jenny had started a fire.

Matt couldn't put it off any longer. He had to go in there and drag her back home to the Sheltering Arms.

Hank might be a friend, but he was also their employer. The little idiot needed to apologize for the argument she'd started with Hank's guest, Amy.

He turned off the engine and jumped out of the truck.

In the few seconds it took him to cross the muddy path between the truck and the veranda, the wind picked up, bending the trees beside the house horizontal and soaking him to the skin with driving rain.

The aged floorboards creaked beneath him with every step he took. He had to put effort into pushing the warped door while it groaned its resistance before finally opening.

The hairs on the back of his neck stood up. He hadn't been in here since his parents had died. What was that? Ten years ago? The living room hadn't changed one bit, except for the woman standing in front of the fireplace.

Jenny kept her back to him, ignoring him when he knew he'd made enough noise entering to rouse the dead.

Soft candlelight shone on her bare back, lit the threadbare blanket that was wrapped around her and hanging below the flare of her hips. When she bent to arrange her wet clothes in front of the fire, it slipped down to her smooth, round bottom, and anger forged a trail through him.

She had a lot of nerve ruining a perfectly good friendship by growing up. Matt didn't care how unreasonable that sounded.

A gust of wind through the open doorway blew his hat from his head but he caught it in one hand.

The cold air raised goose bumps on Jenny's skin.

Even though the candlelight was too dim for him to be sure, he swore he could see them. But then, he'd noticed everything about her lately, like her curves and the new way she walked, swinging her hips too much.

Feminine curves and cowgirl strength. A stunning combination, never mind that she was feisty and fun, and made him feel bad to the bone.

His horsing-around-buddy was a better person than he could ever be, without even trying. She just was.

And now she was a grown woman.

Matt stepped into the room and slammed the door. The cabin seemed to get smaller, becoming too intimate. He rapped his hat against his thigh, spraying water across the wood floor, and threw it across the room to land on the kitchen table.

Jenny straightened, turned and looked at him with the eyes of a woman. Damn. No longer the kid he could toss into the pond when she got mouthy, she'd started to watch him with awareness, making his skin itch and his groin scream for attention.

Looking at her, he felt that old devil, yearning, swamp him. Yearning for what? For a warm body to sink into? Hell, any number of girls in town offered that regularly. For a comfort that would ease his soul? He could always wander into Reverend Wright's church for that. For…love? No way. No how. For a family? Not in this lifetime.

That yearning had been trailing him for too long. *Quit, already,* he ordered. But it was no use with Jenny standing in front of him looking like a cowboy's dream. Damn.

A flicker in Jenny's eyes echoed his desire.

"Matt," she said, gripping the gray blanket against her chest. It rose and fell with her shallow breaths.

He tried to say her name, but nothing came out. He stepped toward her. His boots hit the floor too loudly in the quiet room.

He finally admitted what he'd been denying to himself. That he'd been aware of her growing up not in the last couple of months, but in the last few years. She'd been calling to him and he'd done his best to hide from her.

Jenny stared at him with heat in her eyes, with smoky knowledge and a woman's desire.

Lately, she'd been trying to reel him in like a calf at the end of a rope, but he was too smart for that. He'd resisted her. But here? Now? When she stood in front of him like a slice of heaven on earth?

"You play with fire, kid, and you're going to get burned." His throat hurt, sounded raw.

"I'm not a kid," she said. "I'm twenty-two."

She dropped the blanket and air hissed out from between his teeth. His gaze shot around the room, trying to look at anything but her, but in the end, he was only human.

Her thick braid fell over her shoulder to tease the nipple of one of her breasts. He groaned. Those breasts. Those mile-long legs.

He tried to be noble. "We're friends, Jenny. This could ruin it." He forced his lungs to expand and inhaled the scent of lilacs. God, she was beautiful. "I know about these things. You don't."

"I want to be more than friends, Matt."

A sheen of sweat broke out on his upper lip.

Itchy and unsettled and angry, he yanked her toward

him. Roughly. Her breasts hit his chest, warm through the damp denim shirt.

She wanted to be a woman? Fine, he'd treat her like one.

Matt settled a hand on her hip. He'd held a lot of women in his time, but Jenny's skin was softer than any he'd ever touched.

She opened her mouth to speak, but he didn't want to talk. He brushed one eyelid with a featherlight kiss then moved on to her cheek, and the corner of her mouth. She shivered.

"No regrets, Jenny," he said, his voice husky. "This is sex. Nothing more."

"I want you, Matt," she told him. "What do you want?"

He felt the long-denied truth a split second before he said, "This," and his mouth came down on hers, heavy and demanding.

A rough exhalation escaped him. He braced his arm across her back and crushed her to him, forcing his erection against her belly.

Jenny breathed one word. "Yes."

He spread the blanket on the floor and brought her down with him. He lay on his back and pulled her to kneel above him so he could watch the firelight pour over her curves like molten caramel. While the windows rattled with the violence of the storm outside, the fire sent shadows leaping across the walls.

Jenny unbuttoned Matt's shirt while he unzipped his pants.

She smiled. He reached up to taste that smile.

Wrapping his arms around her, he gave her every particle of himself, taking as much as she had to offer.

When he entered her, he felt like laughing, crying, shouting from the mountaintops.

Jenny came apart in his arms then lay against him as trustingly as a newborn kitten.

Matt followed her into a nameless bliss, found peace, and whispered, "I love you."

Get out of here.

Firelight limned the ancient furniture Matt knew too well.

Run.

He couldn't breathe.

I love you?

Where the *hell* had that come from? It was a god-damn lie, just like everything else in this hole he'd grown up in.

Jenny lay sleeping beside him. Maybe she hadn't heard. She must have.

She craved a family. Damned if he'd hang around to fulfill her dreams. He couldn't do it.

He should have stopped this, should have left it at friendship. Sex *always* screwed things up.

He pulled his arm out from under her head and sat up. He looked frantically around the room. Shadows of bad memories danced in the corners, thickening the air, choking him.

Bile rose in his throat.

Get the hell out of here.

No way did Matt do the white picket fence, the vows at the altar and the "I'll love you forever" crap. No way did he do *kids*.

Marriages ended badly. With a bang.

I love you. What was he thinking?

The fire had long since died, and now the candle flickered out. Darkness pressed on his lungs.

Matt dressed in the dark, his fingers thick and clumsy. He fumbled on the table for his hat, slammed it onto his head and stepped toward the door. The floor creaked.

When Jenny rolled over, his throat constricted, and he felt that marriage noose tighten around his neck.

She sighed, still asleep.

With shaking hands, he pulled on his boots. Opening the door a crack, he squeezed out then rushed through the storm and climbed into the Jeep, the lowest of the low, a jerk.

A coward.

He'd never promised Jenny he was anything other than that, any better than his father or his grandfather before him. Long men didn't do responsibility.

He couldn't have been more honest. *This is sex. Nothing more.*

But was it only sex?

Aw, shut up.

When he roared out of the clearing and across the prairie, the Jeep sprayed rooster tails of mud and water.

Sayonara, Jenny.

Five years later

JENNY LIFTED another forkload of hay into Lacey's stall. She had mucked out too many stalls today, fed too many horses. Her muscles throbbed with the strain.

She'd been exhausted lately, doing both her jobs and Angus's.

Angus hadn't even turned out for the branding last

week. Jenny had handled it all, had called in friends and local teenagers to help with the job. It had been a big one. They'd had a good crop of calves this year.

Maybe soon, he would feel up to doing more around the ranch. He'd been grieving for his dead son for a long time, a couple of years now. It was time to rejoin the land of the living.

The low rumble of a pickup truck caught her attention as the vehicle pulled into the Circle K's yard.

Jenny tossed her rake against the wall and stepped outside, happy for the break until she recognized that black truck and the horse trailer behind it.

Her heart writhed against her ribs.

Why was Matt Long in this corner of Montana five years after he'd left?

She'd hoped never to see him again.

When he stepped out of the truck, still as gorgeous as ever, Jenny's traitorous heart twitched, but she forced it to settle down. Fast.

Shallow charm and a killer grin wouldn't turn her head this time. She'd learned her lesson when he'd run out on her.

He could no longer set her on fire. The only thing that burned for him within her now was anger.

His five-year absence hadn't been anywhere near long enough for her to forgive him.

Had he heard the news? Was he here to mess it all up for her? She wouldn't put it past him.

"What are you doing here?" she asked, striding to within a couple of feet of him, not a trace of welcome in her voice.

He slammed the truck door, then saw her. His mouth

dropped open then closed just as quickly. The line of his jaw hardened.

"What are *you* doing here?" he asked in return, leaning against the door of the truck, crossing his arms. "Thought you'd still be working for Hank on the Sheltering Arms. You just visiting here today?"

His mirrored sunglasses shielded his eyes.

She needed to see them, to figure whether he was a better man than he used to be. Not that it mattered to her. She should have never trusted the rat. Matt, the rat.

"I work here." She stepped closer.

"Since when?"

"Four years now."

He didn't comment, just brushed past her and opened the back doors of his horse trailer. Masterpiece let out a demanding whinny. They must have been on the road awhile.

"You have a lot of nerve coming back to Ordinary," she said. "Especially after the way you left. You couldn't have said goodbye? Or left a note?"

He shrugged.

No conscience.

Once a rat, always a rat.

Good to know. She wouldn't feel guilty about the decisions she'd made anymore. She'd been right to do what she'd done and the hell with Matt's feelings. They weren't her concern.

Matt backed Masterpiece out of the trailer.

Master nudged his chest and Matt took a caramel out of his shirt pocket, unwrapping it. The horse picked it up from Matt's palm with the delicacy of a surgeon.

Jenny still didn't know what he was doing here, and

really didn't care, but she was booting him off this ranch.

"Load Master right back into that trailer," she ordered, her tone so cold her tongue got frostbite. "Get out of here."

"Nope," he said, ignoring her as if she were of no more consequence than a flea. "I take my orders from Angus, not from a ranch hand."

"What are you talking about? What orders?" Dread circled around her belly. Why would Angus be giving Matt orders? "Why are you here on the Circle K?"

"Angus hired me."

No way. She stared at Matt. No *freaking* way.

"You're kidding, right?"

"Nope." He raised his eyebrows at her tone. "What business is it of yours?"

She'd gotten over him years ago, but she sure didn't want to work with him. Never again. And what about Jesse?

Jenny leaned forward, getting into Matt's space. He smelled good. He still used the same aftershave and it brought back memories. Those memories were tainted, though. They weren't the gorgeous dreams she'd wanted with Matt when she was a teenager.

But then, adolescents weren't always the smartest creatures, were they?

Matt had forced Jenny to become a realist overnight. To start planning. She would never again be a dreamer. "Angus wouldn't have hired you without consulting me first."

"Why would he ask you who he's allowed to hire?"

"I'm ranch foreman."

Matt's jaw dropped. "You?"

"Yes, me." She smiled meanly. "He didn't tell you?"

"Why aren't you still on the Sheltering Arms?"

What could she possibly say? That they'd worked there together for too many years? That after he'd run away it had hurt her to stay, to see him in every corner, to picture him on Master racing with her across the prairie? That she'd missed him every minute of every waking hour, and that they had all been waking hours?

She hadn't eaten or slept much for weeks until she'd discovered she had something worth living for, worth fighting for. She'd gotten over Matt pretty damn quickly after Jesse was born.

When she left Sheltering Arms, Angus had given her a job on the ranch he'd bought after her parents had gone bankrupt all those years ago.

She'd come home.

"I wanted to come back to my ranch," she said, finally answering his question. "Angus said nothing about hiring *you*."

"Well, he did. I know Angus Kinsey well enough to recognize his voice on the phone."

God, no.

Jenny turned and strode toward the house.

"Where are you going?" The deep timbre of Matt's voice, flavored with anger, washed over her.

"To talk to Angus," she called over her shoulder. "To get this straightened out."

"There's nothing to straighten out. Angus hired me and I'm staying."

"Not if I can help it."

"He owns this ranch. Even if you are foreman, why would he care what you want?"

She suddenly felt good enough to shout. Payback was so sweet. Matt had hurt her badly when he'd abandoned her. Let him hurt for a while.

Jenny paused on the top step of the veranda and turned around slowly, savoring the moment. With enough smug satisfaction to drown a prairie dog, she said, "In two weeks' time, I'm going to marry Angus."

Matt whipped off his sunglasses. She wasn't sure what she saw in those blue eyes, but it wasn't happiness.

Good. She'd gotten to him.

As if sensing his owner's tension, Masterpiece stirred restlessly. Matt rubbed his hand down his neck and the horse settled.

"Angus is old enough to be your father," he said, his voice little more than a growl.

"So what?" Jenny frowned. "He's a good man. He'll make a great husband."

Take that and shove it up your nose.

She slammed the screen door behind her, shaken, letting everything that she'd just hidden from Matt flood through her, anger so piercing it wounded her, fear so deep it shredded her stomach.

Memories so shaming they burned.

This is sex. Nothing more. The cold-hearted bastard had been telling the truth. For him, it had never been more than sex. How could she have been so mistaken about Matt Long?

I love you. She'd heard him say it so clearly, but it had been a lie.

She stared at her trembling hands. If Matt had had

to leave her after their night together, he should have had the good sense to stay away forever.

His timing couldn't be worse.

But she couldn't blame him for this, really. Angus had brought Matt here.

Standing in the hallway, Jenny forced herself to get control of her nerves or she'd rip into Angus with both barrels blazing. He didn't deserve that. He'd been good to her.

Dread balled up in her stomach like undigested steak. Matt couldn't possibly screw things up for her when she was so close to getting everything she'd always wanted in life. Could he?

She needed reassurance. She needed an Angus Kinsey hug.

She found him in the living room.

He stood in front of the lace-curtained window, one arm stretched high and braced against the wall. Obviously, he'd just witnessed the scene between her and Matt. He glanced at her over his shoulder.

Graying temples and the beginning of a soft middle betrayed his fifty-eight years.

He looked tired.

Angus owned the Circle K, but Jenny ran it. For two years, he'd been detached from the ranch. The death of a man's son could kill a lot of things in him. Even the love of his land.

She liked Angus, cared for him deeply.

What she'd felt for Matt had only been lust. With Angus, it was different. They had respect and a deep affection. If her heart sometimes whispered that she wanted more than that, she ignored it.

Angus must have seen something disturbing on her

face. He came away from the window and opened his arms. She rushed into them, burrowing against his big warm chest.

Hold me. Help me. Reassure me. I'm so scared.

"Why, Angus?" The question came out muffled, but she couldn't pull away from him.

"Why what?" His voice echoed against her ear. "What's got you so upset?"

"I don't want Matt Long here."

"Why not? I thought he was a friend of yours. I thought you'd be happy."

"Why did you hire him?" she asked without answering his question.

"He owes me."

Jenny pulled away to look at him. "Owes you? Because you were good to him when he was a teenager?"

"No. That was freely given. This is for paying the taxes on his land for five years while he was away. So he wouldn't lose it."

"You mean he still owns it?" That cabin she wanted to burn to the ground? The one that had witnessed the worst humiliation of her life? Part of her whispered, *and the best night you ever had,* but she suppressed it. The pain on the morning after had far outweighed the pleasure of the night before.

Angus nodded. "I've been paying his taxes, but now that you and I are getting married, I need to get my life in order. I'm organizing my finances and adding you and Jesse to my will."

"So what if Matt owes you money? Why couldn't he pay you back from Wyoming or wherever he was?"

Angus seemed puzzled by the stridency of her tone.

"Ordinary is his home. He should have stayed here all along."

He stepped away from her and led her down the hall to his office. "I'll show you the paperwork. Matt's going to work off what he owes me here on the ranch."

"Didn't you say once that he was doing well in the rodeo? Why can't he pay you from his winnings?"

"He had an accident with a bull."

What? Matt had been injured? By a bull? She'd always thought him...indestructible, but in confrontations between bulls and men, bulls always won. "How badly was he hurt?"

"Bad enough. Broken ribs. Ruptured spleen. Emergency surgery. His rodeo days are over for good. His winnings all went to pay his hospital bills."

"You've been keeping track of Matt over the years?"

"Of course. He's like a son to me."

Angus sat at the desk while Jenny took a chair across from him. He stretched his arms and clasped his fingers behind his head.

"I don't know what happened to make Matt leave Montana but he should have stayed and ranched that piece of land he owns."

Jenny chewed on her lip.

Angus cast her a glance. "Looked like you two were fighting out there." He gestured with his head toward the front of the house. "What was that about?"

She should tell him, now, while they were alone. It would take Angus only a fraction of a second to see the family resemblance when Matt and Jesse stood side by side. It was unfair to blindside him like that.

She took a deep breath and held it. Angus wouldn't

like this. Could she make him understand why she'd never told Matt about his son? Well enough that Angus wouldn't hate her?

She couldn't stand to lose his respect.

"I need to tell you something," she said.

"Okay," he murmured, sitting forward and releasing his hands.

"Matt is…" *Oh, just spit it out and get it over with.* "Matt is Jesse's father."

"Matt?" Angus fell back against his chair as if someone had hit him. His eyebrows nearly met his hairline. "Jesse's father?"

"Yes," she said. "Jesse is Matt's son."

"I never invaded your privacy, never asked who the father was," he whispered, "but why didn't you ever tell me *this?*"

Oh, Angus, don't be disappointed in me. It hurts.

"Angus, I spend most days trying to forget it, forget that I ever had the poor judgment to get involved with him."

Matt's arrival on the Circle K changed so much for Jenny. Everything had been going along fine. She'd finally found the way to make her long-ago dreams of having a family and working the ranch she'd grown up on come true. She would finally have security for Jesse.

Angus scratched his head, as though he was having trouble taking it in. "I can't believe Matt moved to Wyoming. Why didn't he stay here and raise his boy?" His lips tightened. "I thought better of him."

Angus stood and she reached a hand to stop him from leaving the room to hunt Matt down.

"I didn't tell him."

"What?"

Jenny stared down at her fist on her thigh, at the knuckles turning white, and whispered, "I never told him."

Angus leaned forward to get a good look at her face. "Tell me I misheard you," he said, his tone low and harsh.

"You didn't." She couldn't meet his eyes. Sure, she'd had her reasons for not telling Matt, good ones, but Angus might not agree.

"You didn't tell him he had a son and you don't see what's wrong with that?" The sharp edge of his voice grated on her skin. She'd never heard him so angry.

She lifted her chin defiantly. "No, I didn't. I'm not proud of it, but I had to protect my son. I didn't need Matt to be Jesse's father. I didn't want him to be."

"Why not?"

"I couldn't let him hang around for a couple of months or years and then abandon Jesse."

"Matt is a better man than that."

"No, he isn't. Remember what happened when he got Scotty's daughter pregnant? How Matt took off for a month and only returned after Elsa's miscarriage?"

"That's not a fair comparison. He was fifteen and running scared. He must have been twenty-five, twenty-six, when you got pregnant. He would have done the right thing."

Jenny slapped the arm of her chair. "He was still the kind of man to leave a young woman after a one-night stand, in the *middle* of that night, and never bother to find out if she was pregnant." Her voice rose. "He knew we hadn't used birth control."

"It was your responsibility to track him down and tell him."

"True, and I would have if he'd been a different person."

She'd heard him whisper that he loved her and it had set her heart soaring. She hadn't asked, begged or cajoled. He'd offered it freely. She'd thought they were about to get their happy ending and had fallen asleep with a smile on her lips.

What a fool she'd been.

The following morning, Matt had left Montana. Why would he treat his son any better than he'd treated her? He was a man who raised hopes and then dashed them.

"You remember what Matt was like back then—even in his twenties," she said, "fooling around with any woman who showed an interest. Lots of drinking on Friday and Saturday nights. Traveling with the rodeo whenever he could."

"Jenny," Angus said dryly, "you're describing half the single men in the state." He folded his arms across his chest and took his seat again, preparing to argue.

"Yes, but Matt seemed worse. His childhood was so unstable. He ran out on Elsa. He ran out on me. How could I trust him not to run out on Jesse one day?" She needed Angus to understand but couldn't tell him how that "I love you" had been the answer to fantasies she'd woven around Matt for as far back as she could remember, since the first time she'd found him lying under the cotoneaster bushes on the hill, spying on her family and the ranch, his heart full of envy. She knew he'd loved the house and this land us much as she had.

She stood and spread her hands on the desk. "My son

means more to me than anything on this earth. I would protect him with my life. I'm protecting him now."

Angus shook his head. "Matt has a real decent streak inside him."

"I know." That was the part she'd fallen in love with as a girl. "But I don't trust him. Jesse will fall for him and then Matt will leave. That's always been his pattern. I know this in my bones, Angus."

Jenny felt a headache throbbing against the backs of her eyelids. The fight left her and she sat back down.

Angus came around the desk and settled onto his haunches in front of her. He took her hands in his.

"Your fingers are like icicles." He chafed them. "You have to tell him, sweetheart. It's the right thing to do."

She knew that and hated it.

"Angus," she whispered, "I'm so scared. What if Jesse gets hurt?"

"I'll be here. You'll be here. We'll make it all right for him."

"But—"

"Talk to Matt," he urged.

It was a losing battle and she gave in. "I'll go pick up Jesse."

"Where is he? At Hank's?"

She nodded. "Don't tell Matt anything while I'm gone. Promise?"

After Angus agreed, Jenny breathed a sigh and left the house.

Neither Matt nor Masterpiece was in the yard. The truck and trailer stood along the side of the stable. Obviously, Matt thought he was here to stay for a while.

Not if Jenny could help it.

CHAPTER TWO

JENNY JUMPED into her beater car and sped from the ranch.

Ten minutes later, she drove down the long driveway of the Sheltering Arms and pulled up in front of the house. The grounds were neat as a pin, as usual.

She walked to the nearest corral where a couple of mares chewed on the grass under the fence.

Jenny combed one horse's mane with her fingers, and took comfort from the animal's solid bulk.

She liked the simplicity of animals, of dealing with them. They had no problem offering loyalty and then sticking with it.

Children's voices in the stable rose and fell in playful cadence. She thought she heard Jesse's voice among them. He loved playing with the kids Hank brought to the ranch.

Her nerves hummed. Jesse didn't know who his father was. She'd managed to dodge that bullet for four years now. He hadn't asked yet, but he would.

When she and Angus married, she planned to tell her son that Angus was his father. Jesse would be satisfied with that. He loved Angus.

But what about when he got older, old enough to guess differently?

I'll deal with that when it happens.

Jenny blew a soft breath through her lips. She had to believe her marriage to Angus would work.

A mess of poorly dressed kids ran out of the stable. Jenny approached them. Some kids had holes in the toes of their sneakers, or knees worn out of their pants. They all wore baseball caps with Sheltering Arms written across the front. They were inner-city children recovering from cancer and Hank Shelter was giving them three weeks of pure, unadulterated fun. Hank took in a pack of kids every single month, year-round.

Knowing their father's drill by heart, Hank's two children, four-year-old Michael and three-year-old Cheryl, led the pack. When Amy first came to the Sheltering Arms, a small girl was visiting who had become precious to both Hank and Amy. They'd been devastated when she died, and later named their daughter Cheryl in her honor.

Another little boy, with a head full of beautiful blond locks and long blond eyelashes that would do a girl proud, ran with them. Jesse. Jenny's heart swelled, as it always did when she saw him.

"Jesse!" She waved and her son's smile lit up his face. He ran across the yard and threw himself full force into her arms. Jenny caught him, laughing while she stumbled to keep her balance.

Oh, you rare gem. Oh, my little sweetheart.

She hugged the bundle of energy so hard he finally complained.

"Mo-o-om. I can't breathe."

Jenny loosened her grip and carried her son in her arms with his legs wrapped around her waist, like a little monkey.

She waved to Hank and his children.

"Hey, Jenny," Hank called. Sometimes Jenny missed working for Hank. Sometimes she missed working with the children.

That morning after Jenny and Matt spent the night together, Hank had lost a good ranch hand in Matt. A year later, he'd also lost Jenny.

Most days, though, she was happy to be home, on her family's ranch, even if she didn't own it. Yet.

That would change the day she married Angus. Then half of it would be hers, and someday in the future, Jesse and any brothers and sisters Jenny and Angus made for him, would own the whole thing.

"I'm taking Jesse home now. See you later."

Hank waved back.

"Hank's got a baby horse," Jesse chattered. "He let me pet him. Hannah gave us nimistrome for lunch."

"Minestrone?"

"Uh-huh. It was good 'cept for the beans. Mikey said they make him fart."

Jenny chuffed out a laugh.

Jesse fiddled with the gold chain she wore. "I made a friend. Stacey."

Jenny's throat constricted. He was getting so big, no longer looked a toddler, but more a little boy. Too fast. She was in a weird mood today. Off balance because of Matt.

Some days it felt as if she carried the weight of the world on her shoulders. Keeping secrets could do that to a person, but she was about to unburden herself of the biggest one. She hoped she would feel better after that.

As she held her son in her arms, smelling the hot, active-kid scent of him that she loved, she thought, *What*

*am I going to do about you and your father? You were
never supposed to meet him.*

She silently cursed Angus for contacting Matt, Matt
for agreeing to come back, and her parents for losing her
ranch in the first place. She knew she wasn't being rational, so she forced herself to relax, then kissed the top
of her son's head. There were some things well worth
being thankful for.

She shouldn't be angry with her parents. They'd done
their best. Dad had tried everything to save their ranch,
had even started a quarry that had scarred part of the
land.

She shifted Jesse a little higher on her hip and walked
to the car. She should put him down. He was four years
old, after all, but she wanted him close for a few minutes, though.

Matt was back.

What a cowpie-kicking mess. But this was one mess
she was taking care of for good.

UNSETTLED AND TIRED, Matt threw his belongings onto
a bed at the near end of the bunkhouse. Coming back
to Ordinary was harder than he had reckoned it would
be.

Driving in from Wyoming, he'd thought the trip was
long. Then, all of a sudden, he'd arrived and had to face
too much.

He hadn't wanted to see Jenny. He'd planned to steer
well clear of the Sheltering Arms, but she was here on
the Circle K. Worse still, she was foreman *and* she was
marrying Angus. What a snafu.

He'd just seen her drive off the ranch in a small silver

car. At least he'd have a few minutes of peace until she returned.

Matt wanted to forget that night, and that he'd *ever* told Jenny he loved her.

He didn't want to be reminded of how much he'd missed her in the past five years and the friendship they'd had before that night. Nor did he want to admit how much he'd missed this place and how it was all tangled up with his relationship with Jenny.

She'd been his anchor for years, since he was a kid. She'd watched over him. Then they'd had sex, he'd split, and he'd missed her and Ordinary more than he'd thought possible.

Matt wished he could turn around and beat a track out of here, to get away from his love-hate relationship with this community, but he couldn't leave.

He owed Angus too much money. No way could he let him down.

Why not? Angus let you down. He's marrying Jenny.

So what? You were never going to marry her. Jenny and Angus are free to marry each other.

Yeah, but still...

Still what?

I don't know.

He didn't want to have to deal with Jenny, had spent five years purging her from his mind.

A decrepit sofa sat at the far end of the bunkhouse, decorated with brown wagon wheels and rearing horses on graying beige.

Matt sank into its soft cushions that had accommodated too many rear ends over its life, of the men who'd made Angus's ranch their home for weeks, months or years at a time.

He turned on the small TV, flipped through the channels, then turned it off and tossed the remote onto the scratched coffee table.

An ancient olive-green fridge and stove and a deep freezer made up what might be loosely called a kitchen area.

Matt jumped up and left the bunkhouse. After a while, these places all started to look the same, a blur of lumpy beds and cobbled-together secondhand furniture.

He walked across the yard in search of Angus, remembering when he used to come here as an adolescent, hiding on the low hill above the yard, in the stand of a dozen or so cotoneasters across the top. This ranch had come to be a magical place for him, a spot where parents knew how to make happy families.

Lilacs lined one side of the two-story house. Their scent wafted across the veranda. He stepped through the screen door and entered a foyer that was a few degrees cooler than the sunlit yard.

Maybe in some ways it was good to be back. He closed his eyes and inhaled.

It smelled clean, like lemon and potpourri.

Matt had spent time inside this house as a teenager. He'd loved it. Back then, it had smelled like cigars and fried food.

Far as he could tell, nothing much else had changed. The screen door let in a breeze that ruffled dried flowers in an arrangement on a table by the door.

He didn't remember Angus having a fondness for flowers. Jenny's influence, maybe? Naw, not likely.

Jenny Sterling's name was listed under "tomboy" in the dictionary.

He walked down the hall, passing the living room on his right and the dining room on the left, both filled with oversize dark furniture.

He continued down the hall and spotted Angus sitting behind his desk in the office.

"Hey, Angus." Matt stepped into the room, a smile spreading across his face. This man had saved him, had just flat out saved him all those years ago.

Angus glanced up from the books he was working on and grinned when he saw Matt. He came around the desk and they met in a man-hug, right hands meeting in a bone-crunching handshake and left hands slapping each other's backs.

Matt was so damn glad to see Angus. The past five years had been filled with close acquaintances and a lot of strangers. But friends? No. It was good to touch a friend.

"Matt, it's great to see you." Angus's voice sounded rough, wet.

"You, too." Matt moved to pull away, but Angus hung on and Matt started to choke up. He knew why Angus wouldn't let go. Kyle. Matt understood how Angus felt. Kyle had been his friend.

Matt had called after he'd heard about Kyle's death, but this was the first time they'd seen each other since. Now, being on the Circle K, it was all too real.

Before coming back, Matt had understood in his mind that he would never see Kyle again, but here he had to face the truth. Here he knew it in his heart and missed Kyle badly.

Kyle had died a couple of years ago in a ranching

accident, overcome by silo gas when the tractor venting
the silo Kyle was working inside had died, no longer
flushing out the nitrogen dioxide that built up in silos.
The gas could kill in a matter of minutes. Kyle had never
stood a chance.

Matt remembered the day Angus called with the
news of Kyle's death—a Monday. He hadn't felt normal
for a long time after that.

"Great to see you, Matt," Angus repeated. He released Matt and sat back down, his gaze glued to the
papers on his desk.

Angus had aged in five years, with frown lines on
his forehead, a slight bowing forward of his shoulders.
Probably most of it had come after Kyle's death, as if
he had given up on some part of life.

Matt gave Angus a minute to pull himself together
then said, "I was real sorry I couldn't get back here for
the funeral."

"You had your own problems." Angus rested his
elbows on the desk. "How are the injuries? You all
healed now?"

"Pretty much, yeah." Matt sat across from Angus,
pretended a nonchalance he didn't feel and asked,
"Heard you and Jenny are getting married."

"Yeah, the wedding's in two weeks."

"You mind if I ask why you're marrying her?" He
forced himself to sound unconcerned. So what if there
was an age difference? People did it all the time.

"I want a son." Angus raised a hand before Matt
could object. "Sounds foolish, I know. I'll never get
Kyle back, but I'd like to have children again."

Matt nodded. He'd never lost a child, so who was he

to criticize? There was no fighting a man's desires after living through tragedy.

"Jesse reminds me of how much I've lost." Angus stilled and flushed, as though he'd said something wrong.

Who was Jesse? A ranch hand?

"C'mon outside," Angus rushed on and stood, steering Matt with a friendly hand on the shoulder. "Want to show you some of the new equipment I've invested in lately."

Matt knew he was being put off and wondered why. What was the story with Jesse? It didn't matter. Matt was glad to be distracted from more talk about Kyle. It hurt too much.

Angus showed him around the barns and stables, but seemed fidgety, as if he needed to get away. This went on for the better part of a half hour, then Angus said he had to go into town.

Matt sat on the top step of the veranda, watching the dust from Angus's car settle in the quiet yard.

The ranch hands must be out doing chores.

Strange homecoming, this, with Kyle dead and Jenny here and still angry, and Angus happy to see him, but somehow not acting like himself.

Matt didn't like feeling so alone.

It's your own damn fault. You're the one who's made a career out of leaving.

Yeah, but I don't have to like the results.

He should take a look at his parents' land. His land now. See whether the house was still standing.

No. He jerked to his feet and wiped the seat of his jeans. No way did he want to go back there.

He needed to get rid of that house and he could do it without ever seeing it again.

He strode down the hill to get his truck. He needed to take care of business.

Driving along the shimmering road toward Ordinary, Matt's stomach jumped. He hadn't been in Ordinary in five years.

Home.

He tested the word and tasted bitterness on his tongue.

What was new about that? Ordinary, Montana, hadn't had much use for him while he grew up here, so why should he need it now?

The townspeople used to call him "that Long whelp." As if he had any choice who his parents were.

He steered his pickup down Main Street, absorbing details of the town, like the police station, whose hospitality he'd enjoyed a couple of times as a teen. The New American Diner sat placid, no longer new, but still popular, he'd bet. Did they still serve the best club sandwich in the West?

The town basked under a warm May sun and a picture-perfect sky. Matt rubbed the heel of his hand across his chest to ease a weird ache there.

Perversely, he pulled into a parking spot in front of Scotty's Hardware. There were other spots available, but sometimes he had to remind himself of his own shortcomings. It kept his head screwed on straight.

He wondered if Elsa still worked for her dad. He wouldn't be going in to find out.

When he walked past the store window, Scotty glared at him. Bad timing. Too bad the old geezer hadn't retired.

If Matt planned to stay long enough to pay off his full debt to Angus, he would have to face Scotty at some point. He didn't have it in him today, but that day would come.

Farther down the street, he found what he was looking for. A real estate office.

He stepped inside.

Paula Leger looked up from her desk when he entered. She hadn't changed much since high school, had gotten a little thicker in the middle, but not enough to deter from her perky good looks. She wore her hair short these days, frosted with different-colored streaks.

Her eyebrows rose and she smiled. "Hey, Matt, it's been a long time."

"I remember when your dad used to run this office," he said, happy to see a friendly face. Paula had always been a decent person, fair and more mature than the rest of the kids in their high school class. He didn't remember her ever calling him names or putting him down.

"He still does," she said. "We're partners now. What can I do for you?"

Matt smiled. No bad vibes here. He took a deep breath and then spit it out, trying to do the right thing before he had time to wonder whether it actually was the right thing. "I want to sell my parents' house and land."

If Paula felt any surprise, she hid it well. "Okay, sit down and we'll discuss it."

Paula explained how the process would go and how she would determine what she thought the asking price should be, depending on the condition of the house.

"Last time I saw the place, it was in terrible shape," Matt said. "Whoever buys it will just want the land."

"Okay. Do you have a copy of the key?"

"I've never had one," Matt replied. "We never locked the front door when I was a kid. As far as I know, the house is still open."

"Do I have your permission to go inside to appraise it?"

"Sure. Do what you need to do."

A few minutes later, Matt stepped out of Paula's office and breathed a sigh. He'd lifted an enormous weight off his shoulders. He felt scarred by everything that had happened in that house. Now he would never have to face it again.

That was done. At last.

He stopped when he saw the flat tire on his truck. Scotty? He spun to look in the hardware store's windows, but Scotty wasn't there.

It took him fifteen minutes to get the tire off, another ten to roll it down to the mechanic and half an hour to get it repaired, filled and back on the truck.

By the time Matt left Ordinary, he was tired and thirsty.

All in all, his first trip to town had been mixed. Some people were happy to see him and some clearly weren't. It was better than he'd hoped for.

When he reached the ranch, he pulled in behind a compact silver Ford that had had turned in ahead of him from the opposite direction. He recognized Jenny at the wheel.

He parked behind his horse trailer and got out.

Jenny cut the engine and opened her door, watching him steadily.

Nothing friendly there.

She walked around the car and opened the passenger door. Someone really short got out. Jenny led whoever it was over to where Matt stood at the bottom of the hill.

She looked determined, almost combative. "This is Jesse," she said.

Ah, Jesse. Who was he? Who did he belong to?

Jenny didn't say anything else, just stood and watched him silently. What was going on? Kid seemed kind of familiar. Weird. He was too young for Matt to have met him before, though. Not here in Ordinary, anyway.

"Hey, Jesse," he said.

The kid looked up at him with bright blue eyes and said, "Who are you?"

"I'm Matt."

"Are you new?"

"Yep."

"I can show you around." He balanced on one foot. "I know lots of things."

"Yeah? Do you live here?"

"Uh-huh, with my mom."

"Oh? Who's your mom?"

The kid gave him an odd look, then glanced up at Jenny.

Matt studied Jenny and then the child. Where she was dark, with chestnut hair and deep brown eyes, Jesse was fair, with blond curls framing his face and thick light lashes ringing those blue eyes. But Jesse had a smattering of freckles across his nose.

Matt knew without looking that Jenny did, too.

"He's yours?" he croaked. Judging by the boy's

age, she hadn't wasted any time jumping into bed with someone else after Matt left.

Matt got a weird feeling in his stomach. His nerves skittered. He asked a question he suddenly feared. "Who's the father?"

Jenny crouched down in front of Jesse and said, "Head inside the house. Angela made custard today."

"Custard!" he squealed and ran toward the house on sturdy little legs.

She stood slowly, turned around just as slowly, while a pink stain spread on her cheeks.

"He's yours," she said.

CHAPTER THREE

DAMN, ANGUS THOUGHT, what was wrong with him?

Did he have a death wish?

Sitting in his car on Main Street, he was deeply disturbed. It was missing Kyle so badly, and seeing Matt again, a kid who'd become his second son, but who could never replace Kyle.

And finding out that he'd invited to his ranch the man whose son Angus wanted for his own. What a mix-up. If only Jenny had told him earlier, he never would have asked Matt back to work on the ranch.

But you didn't warn her, did you?

She'd had no idea Matt was coming to the Circle K. In retrospect, Angus knew he should have told her, but his mind was too distracted these days.

As if seeing Matt again and missing Kyle and craving another man's son weren't enough to deal with, his approaching marriage weighed on him, too. Only two more weeks. He had to go into that with a clear head and a clean conscience. He had business to start and finish here today.

Angus stared at the Rose Trellis, knowing that *she* was inside. That she was truly back, had taken over her mother's dressmaker's shop and had no intention of leaving.

Moira Flanagan. Her name cut through his veins, landing like a load of asphalt in his gut.

You're insane coming here like this.

He had no response to that, no argument. His knuckles turned white on the steering wheel, his grip brutal but ineffective. He knew he was going to get out of the car and head on in there to see her.

He stepped out like a man heading to his execution.

Thirty-five years later, the thought of Moira still had the power to move him.

They needed to talk.

Dresses made from rose-printed material hung in the shop window. Lavish. Like Moira.

Since she'd come home for her mother's funeral, Angus had seen her only from a distance. She hadn't left town afterward, though, as he'd expected her to.

Yesterday, he'd heard that she'd taken over her mother's business in town.

He had to see her.

I'm not ready.

You've left it long enough. Get it done.

He exhaled until there was nothing left in his lungs but regret.

He grasped the knob of the front door. Forcing himself to push it open, he stepped inside, setting off a chime somewhere above his head.

The interior was dim after the bright sun outdoors, so he stood still to let his eyes adjust—and to give himself time to steel his heart.

Dresses lined one wall. The other wall was bare.

"I'll be right with you," a musical voice sang out from behind a curtain at the back of the store, deeper and huskier than he remembered from his youth, but still instantly recognizable.

It stirred memories. Desires.

The curtain flew aside and Moira stepped into the room, smiling.

She stopped when she saw Angus, the smile fading from her pale face. He drank in the sight of her. The wide neckline of her dress bared her white shoulders. She'd been a wisp of a girl back then, with breasts too big for her frame. She'd grown into a woman, and age had added substance to the rest of her body.

Lord, what a woman. He had it bad for her. Still.

He curled his fingers into fists.

Don't touch. You've got a good woman at home you're going to marry in two weeks.

Then what are you doing here?

Clearing the air.

He stepped toward her.

She stiffened. "What are you doing here?"

He stopped. The air around her swirled with tension and the scent of her rose perfume.

"Hel—" His voice didn't work, came out as a deep croak. He swallowed and tried again. "Hello, Moira."

"I asked you what you're doing here." Her tone was no longer musical, but thin with distress.

"I thought we should meet. Privately. Before we have to do it in public."

"At your wedding." Her mouth was flat. "I don't plan to attend."

He heard the resentment in her statement and his temper flared.

"You've got no right to be bitter. You left me."

"I know what I did." He wasn't sure what emotion ran

through her voice. Was there regret beneath the anger? He hoped so, hated like crazy to think he'd been the only one in love all those years ago.

"She's so young. Do you love her?"

He couldn't lie. "No."

Her green-eyed gaze shot to his face.

"I care for her, though," Angus continued. "A lot. She's a good woman."

Moira fingered the ribbon on a hat on a table. "But if you don't love her, why marry at all—especially someone so young?"

"Children." His voice shook with fury. "They should have been yours. *Ours.* They should be full-grown and working our ranch."

"Yes," she hissed, whirling away from him. She placed her hands on the counter and hung her head, the nape of her exposed neck unbearably vulnerable.

"Why did you come back?" he asked. *Why are you here to turn my life upside down?*

She refused to look at him, so he studied the top of her head and the once-scarlet hair that had faded to the color of a copper samovar.

"I came home for Mother's funeral last month, and decided to stay."

"Why?" he asked. "There was a time when you couldn't wait to shake the dust of Ordinary off your shoes."

Moira glanced up at that, but her gaze skittered away and she shrugged. The neckline of her dress slipped lower on one shoulder. Her porcelain skin used to fascinate him, white and flawless against the calluses of his tanned rancher's hands. Judging by the tremor running through him, she still bewitched him.

With careful movements he stepped closer to her.

"Was it only me in love all those years ago?" he asked. "Did you ever love me?"

She clasped her hands, but he could still see them trembling. "Always. I've never stopped loving you," she blurted defiantly. "Make of that what you will."

It felt as though a slab of concrete had fallen on him, crushing his chest. "But— You never wrote. Never called. I never heard from you."

Angus gently touched her arm and she pulled away from him.

"Of course I didn't write," she answered. "You married another woman."

"Did you think I'd stand around? I waited for you to come home. I waited for *three years*."

His hand struck the counter. "You could have called anytime in those years before I got married."

He was shaking. "I waited to hear from you. I waited and waited and waited. Why didn't you call?"

"You could have called me."

"*You* left *me*, Moira. It was up to you to let me know if you ever wanted to see me again."

"Oh, Angus, I was busy." When he would have spoken, would have lambasted her for such a flimsy excuse, Moira raised a hand. "New York is like a wild animal, absolutely voracious. It chews up young people and their hopes and dreams and spits them out ruined. I refused to be one of the ruined, one of the losers. I worked my butt off to succeed."

Her defiance left her and she looked fragile, tired.

"Did you succeed?" he asked softly.

"Beyond my wildest dreams."

"Was it worth it?"

"I don't know."

"What does that mean?"

The door chime rang and Angus flinched.

Go. Get the hell out, whoever you are. I'm not finished here.

He watched Moira wipe moisture from her eyes, subtly enough that he was pretty sure the customer behind him wouldn't notice.

He turned around. Norma Christie. Jesus, it only needed this. Crusty Christie, the biggest blabbermouth in town.

"Hello, Moira," she said. "Angus." She inclined her head, unbending that steel rod of a backbone enough to acknowledge him. She'd seemed old when he was young. She was downright ancient now. And judging by the spark in her eyes, just as nosy as ever.

Angus set his jaw. Moira turned around, her face composed, but he could see the strain in her eyes.

"What are you doing in here, Angus?" Norma gestured to the rose-patterned fabrics scattered around the shop. "You getting a dress made for someone? Your fiancée?"

Angus froze. What the heck was he supposed to say? That he had come in only to see Moira? When he was getting married in two weeks? Knowing Norma, she'd put an interesting spin on it and would spread it to half the town. It would crush Jenny if she heard. If there was one thing he knew about Jenny, it was that she valued loyalty above all else.

"Last time I checked," Norma said, "the groom wasn't supposed to order the dress for the bride. He wasn't even supposed to see it before the wedding day."

The dress. He'd forgotten. Moira was making Jenny's wedding dress. How did Moira feel about that?

He couldn't come up with a lie for Norma.

Not one goddamn word.

He saw Moira swallow, watched her pretty throat move and her full lips part.

"Angus came to pick up Jenny's dress, but it isn't ready yet."

She turned to Angus and smiled. It looked like a struggle. "Tell Jenny I'll get those pleats she wanted sewn in right away. It will only be a couple of days."

"Will do." Angus nodded at Norma and left the store, so frustrated his jaw hurt. He didn't feel any better now than when he'd walked into the store. One way or another, he would find out what had happened to Moira over the years and why she'd decided to stay in Ordinary now.

And why the hell she'd never stopped loving him, yet hadn't done a single thing about it in all these years.

MATT KNEW HE'D HEARD wrong. Jenny couldn't have just said that the boy who'd been standing in front of him was his son. He had to have heard her wrong.

She looked serious, though.

"What?" he asked, hoping against hope that he *had* got it wrong. He felt light-headed, as if he was at the bottom of a deep, deep well, with only a small circle of light at the top and someone leaning over and whispering strange things. He couldn't hear properly. *"No way."*

"Yes, he's yours," Jenny said from the top of that long tunnel. "Born nine months and three days after the night we spent together."

A shiver ran across the back of his neck. A wave of dizziness left his skin clammy, as though he'd just walked a mile through a thick fog.

He had a son. A child.

Whooh. He exhaled through his dry lips.

He had a child.

Christ, what was he supposed to do about it? How on earth was he supposed to deal with a child?

Hoo-boy.

His feet started to itch, like he needed to run. But he couldn't leave. He had a son.

He was the boy's father, beyond a shadow of a doubt. Jesse looked familiar because Matt saw a more mature version of that face in his mirror every day.

He was a father.

His legs threatened to give out on him. He broke out in the kind of sweat usually caused by nightmares or rotgut alcohol.

The screen door slammed and Jesse came out with a small Tupperware container and a spoon in his hand. He sat on the top step and shoveled something into his mouth.

That little guy had sprung from his loins.

Afternoon sunlight glinted off the golden hair the boy had inherited from Matt.

Matt had inherited that from his own father—the dad who would never, not in a million years, have been voted Father of the Year.

Deserter of the Year, more like.

Or Drunk.

Or Layabout.

Or Wife Beater.

One hell of a frickin' package.

The old confusing, crushing amalgam of feelings flooded him—love, hatred, admiration, sorrow, hero worship. Disappointment.

Matt stared at the child on the veranda.

I am a father.

His body couldn't decide what it wanted to do, whether he should run scared or cry like a baby.

"Why didn't you tell me?" he asked, his voice as cold as the water at the bottom of the well he was drowning in.

"I know you, Matt. You don't have staying power." Jenny looked stoic, heartless, so sure in her opinions of him.

"You never gave me the chance," he said.

"Sorry, Matt. My first responsibility is to Jesse. If that means protecting him from his own father, I'll do it."

Matt's chest burned. She thought so little of him. Who had ever had faith in him? So few people.

Angus. Jenny at one point, but no more.

Maybe he should leave, figure out another way to pay Angus back. But he knew he couldn't leave.

He had a son.

He shouldn't have come here. Life was too complicated here, even worse now that he knew about Jesse.

"You can't tell him," Jenny said.

"What?"

"You can't tell him you're his father."

Something inside his chest ached. Pride, he guessed, or was it something deeper? Ownership?

"If you tell him and then leave," Jenny continued, "he'll be so badly hurt."

He shouldn't have come back to Ordinary. And if he'd had any other option, he never would have.

A thought occurred to him. "Wait a minute. You're marrying Angus. Were you just going to let him become the boy's surrogate father?"

"Yes. We both know he makes a good one."

"Why wouldn't you tell me first before doing that?"

Jenny bit her bottom lip and appeared to be struggling with what she had to say. "I need a dependable man to be Jesse's father."

"And I'm not," Matt said bitterly.

Jenny clenched and unclenched her hands. "No," she said. "We both know you aren't."

That hurt.

She must have realized it because she stretched one hand toward him then let it fall. "Angus will be a better father than you. He's the better man for Jesse, Matt."

Jenny seemed regretful, but Matt couldn't stand to look at her a second longer, to stand in the same yard with her. Even if he was a coward at heart, even if she didn't respect him, she should have told him the truth.

He should have known he had a son.

She shouldn't be giving his child to another man to raise.

On one level, he barely recognized that he was angry with her for getting pregnant in the first place, for making him feel responsibility when he didn't want to, as if there hadn't been two of them having sex that night.

Matt turned his back on Jenny and strode to his truck, angry, afraid, too unsettled to know exactly what he was feeling. Shocked, definitely.

Man, oh, man, he hadn't been prepared for this kind of problem. Since that scare with Elsa, he'd been really careful with birth control. So what had happened that night with Jenny? He hadn't given it a single thought— had only felt that he needed her, and that he had to have her.

He'd lost control.

He started the engine, made sure the kid was still sitting on the veranda and then took off down the driveway, not caring how much noise he made. When he hit the highway, he revved the engine and burned rubber.

He didn't know where he was going, only knew that he had to get away to clear his head.

I am a father.

As Matt neared the turnoff to his parents' house, he slammed on the brakes, hitting the gravel shoulder in a spray of fine stone and dust, and fishtailing. He missed the dirt road that led into his property.

Breathing hard, he took off his hat and threw it onto the seat beside him.

He didn't have a clue where he needed to go or what he needed to do, but maybe it was no accident that he'd braked before he'd made any firm decisions.

Putting the truck into reverse, he backed up and turned onto the old road. Rainstorms had washed ruts into the dirt, and the truck bounced off them as he drove.

He approached the house and tried to dredge up a memory, any memory, that wasn't bad. Not of Jenny and him and their night together, though. That memory was good and bad and insane. At this moment, he didn't want to think of her, not when he wanted to hurt her so badly for the way she'd hurt him, for what she'd taken from him.

His boots rang loud and hollow on the porch floor, and he sidestepped a hole. The door groaned like an old woman. Then he was inside the house and lost in memories of his childhood.

He closed the door behind him, to keep the bugs out and the really tough memories in. On second thought, he opened it again, hoping against hope that all the memories would fly out, leaving nothing more than a house. But they refused to leave. They buzzed around his head like mosquitoes ready to draw blood.

The stone fireplace still dominated the small living room and open kitchen.

An ancient Christmas tree, brown and desiccated, stood in the far corner. Silver balls and bits of tinsel hung on it. His mother's last attempt at making this place a home?

Matt held himself rigid, afraid of the emotions that would flood out of him if he let them. They threatened to drown him.

Keep it cool, Matt. Keep it cool.

He spotted a bunch of dust-coated mail on the Formica table by the door. Matt had left it there, unopened, after his parents had died. Other than he and Jenny that one night, no one had been here since then. He flipped through what was left of his parents' lives.

He picked up one large manila envelope, then stilled. He didn't have to guess what it was. He already knew. The autopsy. No, thanks. No, no, no. He dropped it back onto the table and stalked into what had been his bedroom. Not one clue to his personality existed in the room—no posters nor CDs nor photos. Nothing. No

Matthew Long. He'd spent his adolescence avoiding the homestead.

Kyle's room had been messy, with football posters on the wall and a computer and his own TV and *Playboy* magazines under the bed.

Matt avoided his parents' room, couldn't possibly go in there, so headed back out to the kitchen.

He touched the stove and left his fingerprints in a layer of dust. When had it last been cleaned? More than fifteen years ago. Just before she died, Mom had been consumed by her anger and depression. The house had become more and more dirty, until Matt couldn't stand to eat there.

He opened a cupboard door and spotted a tin of beans and a loaf of bread, now green and dried out. He opened another cupboard door and froze. There on the second shelf, beside the salt and pepper and a bag of pasta, was a small, framed photo of his mother and him.

He looked younger than Jesse was—maybe four, maybe only three. Why was it in the cupboard? Did she want to look at it every time she reached for the saltshaker? Or had she put it here without realizing? Like when he used to find the milk, warm and sour, in a cupboard, and unopened tins of beans in the fridge?

His mother was holding him in her arms and smiling. She'd been so pretty when she was young.

Flashes of memory filled his head, glimpses of this and that, with no rhyme or reason, before finally settling on this one. He thought that maybe he remembered when this photo had been taken.

He remembered his shock later, after his mother had changed.

"MATTHEW, WHAT IS THIS?" Mama held up a pair of pants with holes in the knees. He'd put them in the laundry basket on the floor of his closet, with all his other dirty clothes, just the way he was supposed to.

"Well, what do you have to say for yourself?" Her voice sounded funny, like one of the bad ladies in the Cinderella movie. She sounded mean.

"Those are my jeans."

"I know that, you little moron."

His mouth dropped open. Mama called him a name. She never did that before.

"I mean, why do they have holes in the knees?"

He shrugged. "I don't know. I must have fallen down."

She hit him across the face. He fell on the floor and cried. Where was the mama he liked? Where was the mama who loved him?

MATT CAME OUT of his memory with the question he'd asked himself so many times as a child. Where was the mama who loved him?

It had started the day she'd slapped him and had gone downhill from there, with Mama becoming more and more demanding, her demands more and more unreasonable.

Then Pop started to stay out later and later, coming home only long enough to make sure his kid idolized him and then running off to another rodeo or another ranch or another bar.

To another woman, Missy Donovan from Ordinary.

When Pop did come home, he was angry and drunk and ready to leave again, but not before he and Mama tore each other apart in the bedroom. They went at it like animals.

When Matt was old enough, he got out of the house before they started, and stayed out until long after they finished.

Matt's shell threatened to crumble now, to let the emotions free to kill him with their poison.

He set the old photo on the scarred countertop, face-down because he couldn't stand to look at him and his mother happy. What kind of weird compulsion had driven a warm, loving woman mad?

Was it inside him, too? Was there some sort of double curse in his life? He'd learned too much of the wrong things from his father. Love 'em and leave 'em. Don't let a woman get her hooks into you. When things get too tough, run scared.

Was he also eventually going to lose his mind the way his mother had?

And now he had a child to worry about.

What on earth had he ever learned here that would help him to be a parent?

JENNY HAD BEEN POSITIVE Matt would run, had known it in her marrow. Then why did she feel so disappointed that he had? It was nuts. She didn't want Matt sticking around or deciding that he should have a hand in rais-ing her son.

She and Angus would do just fine raising Jesse. Angus knew how to be a good father.

She sat down on the top step beside her son and took the small spoonful of custard he offered her.

"Do you want to play in the backyard when you're

finished?" she asked, smoothing his bangs away from his face.

"Yeah." He lapped up more of his custard.

Angus drove into the yard in his big silver Cadillac. When he got out, he looked tired. Frustrated.

As she'd done so many times lately, Jenny wondered what was going on with him. What was distracting him? He approached the veranda with heavy steps.

His face lit up for Jesse, though.

"Hey, little buddy," he said and tickled the boy.

Jesse giggled then offered him custard.

"No, thanks. You finish it." Angus turned his attention to Jenny. "How did it go?"

"About as well as I expected. He lit out of here twenty minutes ago. Barely hung around long enough to find out his name." She tipped her head toward her son.

Jesse finished his custard.

"Take the container to Angela in the kitchen and head out back," Jenny told him. "I'll be there in a minute."

The screen door slammed shut behind him. Jenny smiled. Kids made so much noise.

Angus put one foot on the bottom step. On his face, Jenny read a disappointment in Matt that ran much, much deeper than her own.

Angus had always wanted to think the best of Matt, and he hadn't had Jenny's firsthand experience with Matt's leaving.

"Angus, I hate to say 'I told you so,' but this is exactly what I expected."

"Where did he go?"

"I haven't a clue."

Angus glanced around the grounds. "I guess he'll come back for his stuff later."

Jenny smiled grimly. "Oh, yeah, he'll be back for Master."

He didn't think twice about leaving me behind, but he would never forget his horse.

"Then he'll go for good," she continued. "I'm sorry, Angus."

Angus mounted the stairs and rested a heavy hand on her shoulder. If she could ease his disappointment, she would, but the truth was the truth.

She stood and walked around to the backyard where Jesse played on the jungle gym. She helped him across one part that his arms weren't long enough for.

Jesse put his small feet on her shoulders and she held his waist. They'd played this game so many times in the past year, but they never grew tired of it.

Jesse squealed and giggled and Jenny laughed. The world felt right again.

Matt knew about his son now, but he wouldn't stay. Jenny could get on with her plans. She could marry Angus and raise her son on the ranch that was in her blood, that she'd wanted to live on her whole life.

She used to sit up by the cotoneasters as a child and look down on the ranch with such a swell of pride, knowing that someday it would all be hers.

Her dreams had started when she was little more than nine or ten. At the time, her world spun on an axis that was sure and constant.

Her parents loved her. One day, she would have a nice man like Daddy to love her. They were going to build a house on the banks of Still Creek.

Mom and Dad had shown her the piece of land they would give her. It was beautiful. She would raise her family there until the house felt too cramped.

Then they would all move to the big house and Mom and Dad would take the smaller house in the clearing by the stream.

Jenny would live on the ranch her entire life, as her Sterling forefathers had done before her and as her children would do long after.

Then they'd lost everything.

Bankruptcy.

Her heart had broken.

She'd lost hope for many years, but things were finally, blessedly right. Everything would be fine.

Jenny heard a noise behind her. Thinking it was Angus or the housekeeper, she turned with a smile.

Matt stood by the back fence.

Her smile fell away.

The look on Matt's face terrified her.

He watched her and Jesse play with pure, unadulterated longing. He watched his son with hunger.

"I'm staying to get to know him." He turned and stalked away and Jenny's world turned to dust.

CHAPTER FOUR

MATT SAW ANGUS step out of the house, so he walked over to confront him. Why hadn't Angus ever contacted him, told him that he had a son? The betrayals kept mounting.

Maybe he hadn't known.

When he noticed Matt, Angus's expression turned grim. Matt's hope fell. Angus *had* known.

"You knew and you never called me?" Matt asked, a world of accusation in his voice.

"I found out only after you got here today. Jenny came and talked to me." He set his hand on Matt's shoulder. "How are you doing?"

Matt's teeth hurt. He struggled to relax his jaw. "I don't really know. I didn't have the greatest role model. I don't have a clue what to do with the boy."

"Give it time," Angus said. "It will come to you."

Matt wasn't sure about that, but he'd stick around to find out. After he'd paid his debt to Angus, he'd see how things were going with the kid.

In the meantime, he had to deal with his anger toward Jenny. Didn't Angus think it was wrong of her not to tell him?

"How can you still want to marry a woman who would keep a child from his father? Who would lie to a man about something that important?"

"Matt—" Angus cleared his throat. Whatever he had to say was clearly painful to him. "She wouldn't have lied to me. She wouldn't have had reason to."

That hurt, but Angus was right.

Matt had earned his reputation fair and square, and now had to face the consequences.

"Angus!"

A happy shout from the side of the house had both men turning their heads. Jesse barreled across the clearing and threw himself against Angus's knees.

Angus picked him up and tossed him into the air, catching him effortlessly on the way down. He had a great love for children. Too bad his wife had died before they'd had more than one.

Now that one was dead.

Matt watched Angus with Jesse and wondered if he was trying to replace Kyle with the boy.

"I petted a new horse today." The pipsqueak had a high voice.

Angus turned to Jenny with concern on his face and Matt could tell it was to see how she was doing after confessing to him.

For God's sake, Angus shouldn't be worried about Jenny. He should be worried about Matt. Only Matt. He was the one who'd been wronged. Not Jenny. She could have called him at any time in the past five years.

Jesse took Angus's face in both of his hands and turned Angus's attention back to himself. "Hank says I can go in the pool on the weekend if it's warm enough. Wanna come?"

"Sure." He put the boy down, but as Jesse turned away and headed for the house, Angus stared down at him with his heart in his eyes, full to overflowing with affection, but Jesse wasn't Angus's son. He was Matt's, and Matt hadn't had the same time to get to know him as Angus had had.

Had Angus bathed Jesse when he was a baby, changed his diaper, fed him? Had he done all of the things Matt could have done with his son?

Jesse babbled to Angus as if they were best friends.

On his way past Jenny, Angus wrapped his arm around her shoulders and the three of them walked into the house like a real family, leaving Matt feeling like an outsider.

Story of my life.

Matt felt his jaw tighten again as though someone was screwing it on too tightly. He loved Angus, didn't want to be jealous, didn't want to resent his relationship with Matt's son and Jenny, but he did.

Why? You don't want Jenny for yourself and you don't know if you want Jesse in your life permanently.

It didn't matter. It hurt to look at the three of them together.

Matt went to the stable to saddle Masterpiece. He had a bad case of jitters that needed burning off.

In the late-afternoon sun, he rode Master across Angus's fields until they were both worn out.

While he unsaddled his horse, the ranch hands returned. He knew them all—Hip and Will, Hal and Kelly, Jason and Brent. Apparently, there were also a couple of young kids fresh out of high school who came in from surrounding ranches every day, along with a pair from town.

After a round of handshakes and backslaps, they unsaddled and curried their horses and headed off to the bunkhouse for showers.

Just as Matt stepped out of the building, Angus approached.

"Matt, I want you to take your meals in the house with Jenny, Jesse and me."

No way. The last eight hours had been full of enough drama for one day. He'd already noticed the line of picnic tables in the backyard protected by a long canvas awning. Several of the hands were already strolling toward them.

"Do the hands eat in the yard?"

"As often as weather allows. Why? You want to sit with them?"

"Yeah."

"Because of Jesse?"

Jenny, actually, but Matt didn't want to share that with Angus, so he nodded.

Angus returned his nod and went back inside.

Matt headed out to the yard as a stout middle-aged woman came out of the house carrying a tureen of something that smelled spicy.

Angus had a housekeeper these days named Angela.

Dinner was Hungarian goulash and home-baked bread. Seemed that Matt always craved good food, a rare treat in so much of his early life. He wondered if his craving for it would ever die.

If he'd married Jenny years ago, he'd be eating sawdust and hay for dinner. She was a lousy cook. Thank God he'd left.

He looked around Angus's property. Pretty green fields stretched as far as the eye could see. Cattle grazed out there somewhere, getting fat on spring grasses and the feed the crew put out in the fields every morning.

A jungle gym and slide for Jesse made the backyard seem homey.

Angus's ranch hands admired and respected him.

A thought that had always spun around in Matt's head came whispering in again. Why were some people born into good families, good circumstances, while others like himself were born into hell?

Didn't seem fair.

Angela refilled that tureen twice. Matt reached for more.

After dinner, she brought out an enamel pot of coffee with a platter of homemade cookies.

Jenny came out of the house and poured herself a cup. She stood at the end of the table.

Matt tried not to notice her. Hard to do when he sat facing her and the setting sun turned her skin to gold.

A belt was cinched around her middle. Still slim even after the kid, Jenny's waist could probably still fit in Matt's hands. Maybe he should try it to see.

No! Stop those thoughts right there.

"Hal," she said, "how did you and Hip do hauling out that fencing today?"

Hal leaned back, tucking his long fingers into the front pockets of his jeans. "Good. We've got a little more to do in the morning, then we can go wherever you want."

"Take a four-wheeler and a truck and haul a bunch to the edge of MacCaffery's property. I drove out yesterday. A lot of it's been damaged by moose or elk trampling it through the winter."

Hal nodded. "You don't want any of MacCaffery's cattle mixing with ours."

"No telling whether one of their bulls might have venereal disease," she replied. "Last thing we need is to have it spread to Circle K ranch."

Jenny turned to Will. "How about you and Kelly take the land running alongside Sheltering Arms land? I saw a couple of young bulls with broken dicks mixed in with the herd. Bring them in for shipping out. We'll sell those."

Bulls sometimes got too excited with their lady friends and hurt themselves. They weren't worth anything to the ranch if they couldn't impregnate cows.

"Jason and Brent," Jenny continued, "take the old Ford and load it up with salt blocks for the heifers you put out to pasture today."

Jenny gave orders naturally, without bossiness or bravado.

Once the business of the day was taken care of, Jenny raised one hip to sit on the end of the table while she kibitzed with her ranch hands. A soft smile lit her features. She petted the head of an Australian shepherd who rested his nose on her thigh. Matt stood, too quickly, surprising everyone. He had to get away from the sight of that wandering hand and the way it caressed the dog so gently.

MATT STOOD OUTSIDE the bunkhouse and stared up at the stars. Listening to the wind sough across the yard and up the small hill through the cotoneasters, Matt felt a familiar urge.

As a child, he used to run over from his home when he needed to get away and lie up there and spy on Jenny and her family, to watch how a real family should behave.

Later, after the Sterlings had lost the ranch to bankruptcy and Angus had bought it, Matt had spied on Angus and Kyle, to learn how a good father treated his son.

He trudged up the hill now and stood at the top, looking across the ranch. He couldn't see much in the darkness, but staring at the star-dusted dome above his head, he had a sensation that he'd felt up here before, that he was part of something larger than himself. Larger than that hellhole he'd grown up in. Larger than his parents.

He knew what he would see in the daytime. Green fields that spread as far as the eye could see. Shallow blue-purple hills that dotted the skyline.

Somewhere in the distance, his parents' house stood on the land his father had never worked, but it was Angus's ranch, Angus's house, that had always felt like home to Matt.

Below him, the house was dark. Everyone had gone to bed. Matt might have been the last man in the universe.

An owl's hoot drifted on a chilly breeze. Matt smiled and buttoned his denim jacket. He wasn't completely alone. Well, often in his life, he'd felt more comfortable with animals than with people.

Matt lay on his stomach and stretched out on the cool earth, the way he used to when he spied. The spring grass smelled fresh, felt soft. By August, it would be sunbaked and dried. It had always scratched his skin, but he never complained and he never stopped coming.

Matt would watch Angus and Kyle toss a baseball

back and forth while something that smelled like heaven cooked on the barbecue.

The *thwap-thwap* of the ball hitting baseball gloves Matt would die to own had hypnotized him, soothed him. Sometimes, he drifted off to sleep.

The branches and leaves chattering above him in the breeze spoke of those memories, of the first time Angus found him.

THE MAN PRODDED Matt's shin with his boot. "What are you doing up here?"

"Nothin'," Matt mumbled, rubbing sleep out of his eyes. He knew the man's name was Angus Kinsey, though they'd never met. "I ain't doing anything wrong."

"I've got sausages and burgers on the barbecue," Kinsey said. "C'mon down."

Matt's head shot up. He stared at the man. The guy was offering food?

"Why?" Matt eyed him with suspicion. He'd learned a long time ago that no one ever gave something for nothing.

"Because you look like you could use a good meal," Mr. Kinsey answered, his voice and eyes steady.

Matt was no one's charity case.

He was on his feet and heading toward his own land when Kinsey grabbed his jacket from behind and hauled him around to face him. Matt had gained thirty pounds of muscle in the months since he'd turned fifteen. He tried to pull away, but Kinsey was big and wouldn't let go.

Just then, Matt's stomach growled. He hadn't eaten anything since he'd grabbed the last three slices of cheap white bread from the kitchen that morning. He'd had to tear off the moldy corners.

"Put your pride in your back pocket where it belongs," Kinsey said, his voice gruff. "You're hungry and you're going to eat."

He wrapped his hand around the back of Matt's neck, where it felt strong and warm. Pop hadn't touched him like this in years. Kinsey urged him down the hill.

A lean, shiny border collie jumped on Matt. He touched her soft ear.

"That's Gracie," Kinsey said. "Sit and eat."

He shoved Matt onto the wooden seat running along one side of a picnic bench, then pressed down on his shoulders to make sure he stayed put.

Kyle was already sitting at the bench, his shoulders broad like his father's, his hair dark. Matt knew him vaguely from school. They were in the same science class.

Kyle would probably think Matt was a loser for spying, getting caught and coming down here to eat.

Kinsey put sausages on the table, not the skinny cheap tube steaks his mom bought. He could smell the meat in them—all meat, no filler. Then Kinsey put a paper plate covered with hamburgers, an inch thick on fat buns with sesame seeds on top, in front of him.

The food—God, the smell of the food—mesmerized him.

Kyle grabbed a sausage and slammed it onto a bun, squirted it with mustard and said, "Hey, you finished that science project yet?"

Matt shook his head. He didn't do homework.

"You want to work on it together?" Kyle asked with his mouth full.

"Kyle," his dad admonished, but Kyle just grinned, showing bits of hot-dog bun in his teeth.

Mr. Kinsey didn't yell, didn't slap his son upside the head. Just shook his head and sat down at the table and dug into his meal.

Smoke drifted from the barbecue and smelled of charring meat and fat. Matt's mouth watered. His head felt light, like it was gonna float off his shoulders any minute.

Matt didn't know where to start, or how much to take. Kinsey shoved the burgers closer. "Eat," he ordered.

Matt swung his legs over the bench and tucked them under the table. No skin off his nose if the guy wanted to throw food away on whoever happened to trespass on his property.

Picking up a hamburger, Matt bit into it. It sent shock waves through his system. He chewed the meat too fast and swallowed. He wanted to savor it—couldn't—and took another huge bite. When was the last time he'd had a barbecued burger? He couldn't remember. They didn't own a barbecue at home or have money for the diner in town. As he wolfed the burger down, he blinked a lot. A kid would have cried.

When he finished the burger, he wiped his hands on his jeans.

"Here." Kinsey slid a paper napkin across the table.

Matt eyed the sausages. He wanted one bad. Could he just pick it up? Or did he have to stop eating now?

"Go ahead, eat." Kinsey shoved the plate at him.

Matt slathered mustard on the fat sausage, not bothering with a bun, then picked it up with his fork. He bit off one end and juice ran down his chin. He lifted his

arm to wipe his face, caught Kinsey's eye and used his
napkin.

When Matt stood to leave, Kinsey asked, "You play
horseshoes?"

Matt shrugged. "Yeah, I guess."

The three of them threw horseshoes until the light
faded so much they couldn't see the pegs.

Kyle ran into the house, shouting over his shoulder,
"See you at school."

Mr. Kinsey said, "We eat at the same time every
evening."

What was the guy after? Kinsey lived with his kid.
Matt hadn't seen a woman around. Matt wasn't stupid,
could guess what he wanted in return.

"Why don't you have a wife?" Matt blurted.

Pain flickered across the man's features and Matt
knew he'd said the wrong thing.

"She's dead." Kinsey walked away a little and rubbed
his neck. When he came back, he looked sad.

"Listen, kid, I don't want anything from you. You
were hungry, right?"

Matt nodded.

"The food is here if you want it."

"Thanks," Matt mumbled. That was one thing his
loco mother had managed to teach him—please and
thank-you.

Matt turned and left, his spine straight and his shoulders square. He didn't return the next night, or the one
after that, or the next. On the fourth night, though,
Kinsey caught him spying again, watched him from
the front veranda and waved him down. Matt had kept
hidden. How did the guy know he was there?

Matt stood, dusted off his jeans—the only pair he

had without holes in the knees—and ambled down the hill. He wanted to break into a run, to devour whatever smelled so good on the grill, but he forced himself to go slowly. When he reached bottom, he'd stick his pride in his back pocket and sit to eat, but until then he'd take his time, so the man would see exactly who Matthew Long was proud to be.

He ate three hamburgers that night and Kinsey smiled at him. Kyle asked him again to team up for the science project. He said okay.

Matt had realized a long time later that Angus and Kyle had known he was up there spying many months before coming up the hill to get him. That first night they invited him down, Angus had put lots of hamburgers and sausages on the grill to feed the hungry kid that Matt was.

That second evening while Matt was at Kinsey's, Pop came home with two new rodeo buckles and a bottle of whiskey—already three sheets to the wind when Matt returned home after dinner. The house smelled of booze, garbage and stale bedsheets. When Pop pushed Mom into the bedroom with a hot look in his eyes and Mom stared back with that crazy excitement she always had around Pa, Matt ran out of the house.

In the morning, Angus found Matt on the hill wearing only his thin denim jacket, fast asleep and curled around Gracie. The rancher took Matt down to breakfast with him and Kyle.

Matt ate three fried eggs and half a pound of bacon and maybe five, six slices of toast.

Kyle gave him clean clothes for school and Angus made him take a hot shower.

That evening, Kinsey showed him how to bust a bronc. Matt learned a lot from Angus. From Kyle, too.

MATT ROLLED OVER and stared at the moon through the trees. God, he'd missed them.

It was so good to see Angus again, so strange to see the place without Kyle.

Even now, the memories of all the food Angus had served him were so real he could almost taste them. All he smelled, though, was the warm earth beneath him. He picked up a handful of soil and sifted it through his fingers. It gave off a scent of renewal—or decay, depending on how you looked at it.

MORNING BROKE with a bright sun on the horizon and Jenny hummed under her breath on her walk to the stables, stepping through shimmering streaks of gold cast across the yard. She stepped around puddles that a midnight storm had left behind.

The long shadows of the outbuildings held the raw chill of the night's darkness that would soon melt away in the heat of the day.

In the distance, a couple of crew members headed out with feed for the cattle. Good, a nice early start.

The front door of the house opened behind her and she turned. Angus stood on the porch, a coffee in his hand and a distracted frown on his face. Less than half of his mind was on the ranch these days and it worried her. She knew it was leftover grief, but lately, though, just in the last month or so, he'd gotten worse.

Was it the wedding? Was he regretting their agreement?

They both had their own reasons for marrying, but

what if Angus suddenly balked? She'd never get her ranch back.

With a worried frown, she stepped into the dim stable.

A rich tenor rang from inside one of the stalls—Matt, singing an old Dwight Yoakam hit. So Matt was still a big fan. He used to whistle Dwight's songs all the time. She hadn't realized until just now how much she'd missed it.

"A Thousand Miles from Nowhere."

She remembered a line from the song about having bruises on the guy's memory.

Me, too, she thought. *I do, too.*

Thoughts of forgotten wounds got her back up. She'd come to terms with her past and had made plans to move on. She didn't need Matt here reminding her of her scars.

Straightening her spine, she walked down the center aisle and found Matt mucking out Master's stall.

When he saw her, he stopped singing. She stood in the silence, staring at the face she saw reflected in her son every day. Shadowed by his black hat, it gave nothing away.

"You going for a ride?" he asked, his voice husky.

She nodded. "I need to show you around the ranch."

His shoulders stiffened. "I already know this ranch."

"Yeah, but I have to update you on the way things are done these days. Saddle up."

Matt scowled.

"Listen, Long, I'm no happier about this than you

are, but I'm ranch foreman and now you're one of my employees."

"Why can't I take my orders from Angus?" He sounded mulish.

Jenny hesitated then said, "Angus isn't too involved in the running of the ranch these days."

"Why not?"

"Kyle." She didn't have to say more.

"He doesn't care about the ranch?" Matt asked.

"Not like he used to. He's run out of steam, but he's working on getting it back. He'll be okay soon." She hoped like crazy she wasn't lying.

She crossed the aisle to Lacey's stall.

"Where's the boy?" Matt called.

Jenny stilled. "His name is Jesse." She turned her back to him and picked up her saddle. The guy couldn't even remember his son's name?

Matt was silent for a while then asked, "Where's Jesse?"

"He stays with Angela while I work. Sometimes he visits the Sheltering Arms. He likes going there."

Matt didn't respond.

"I spend a lot of time with him," she said hotly. "He doesn't spend all day with her. I take care of him well."

Still Matt didn't speak. She turned to look at him.

He was watching her. "I don't doubt it," he said quietly.

She'd gotten all defensive for nothing. His silence hadn't been any kind of judgment on her as a mother.

For God's sake, calm down. His opinion shouldn't matter to you anyway.

They rode out, Jenny ahead of Matt. She could swear she felt Matt's gaze on her and wished he'd pull up beside her so he couldn't watch her.

CHAPTER FIVE

MATT RODE behind Jenny, studying the woman she'd become.

A rich mahogany braid trailed out from under her beige cowboy hat, falling almost to the belt that was slung around her hips.

The jeans that covered her long legs had been beaten into soft submission by hours in the saddle and lovingly outlined every inch of those strong thighs and calves.

Her youthful promise had blossomed into a ripe maturity. Maybe having the baby had changed her.

They rode the perimeter of the ranch and, from a distance, waved to Will and Hip doing repairs on a fence.

Jenny halted at a point in the fence where the wire had either been trampled or worn down.

"So much of this fence is old. The men spend a lot of their days replacing wire."

Matt pointed to rolls of wire lined up like enormous steel donuts farther along the fence.

"You planning repairs on all the fences?"

"Yeah," Jenny said. "Those should probably be under lock and key."

Matt glanced at her. "Why?"

"They're worth a bit and there've been some thefts in the next county lately. Gasoline for ranch equipment.

Wire for fencing. A cow or two, either for meat or to sell."

"Any idea why?"

"Times are tough." Jenny stared out over the fields. "A lot of families are treading water these days."

"One step ahead of bankruptcy?"

"Yeah. I feel bad for them."

"Angus doesn't seem to be struggling too much." The fact that he could afford to replace a couple of hundred miles of fencing spoke volumes about the state of his finances. "That could cause a lot of envy in a man trying to feed a family. Maybe make him steal from a richer neighbor."

Jenny shook her head. "True, but I can't think of a farmer or rancher around Ordinary who'd stoop so low."

Matt shook his head. "Doesn't seem likely that anyone local would steal. I think your wire is safe."

He turned to smile at her, but she wouldn't look at him. He couldn't blame her. He wasn't any more comfortable with her than she was with him.

Suddenly, Jenny lifted her face, like a dog catching a scent on the wind.

"What is it?" he asked.

"You didn't hear that? Listen."

They sat in silence until Matt heard it, too—a cow lowing somewhere nearby.

"What of it?"

"It sounds like it's near the quarry. It shouldn't be. The cattle are well beyond that."

She took off without warning, leaving Matt in her dust. Not for long, though. He caught up to her, easily. He glanced sideways and saw her grin.

They'd done this all the time when they'd worked on the Sheltering Arms, had broken into races out of the blue, just for the fun of it. Jenny spurred Lacey on, but Matt merely pulled forward, a smile tugging at one corner of his mouth. She was crazy to try to outrun him. Lacey was no match for Master.

She moved into the lead. Matt caught up again. She leaned forward. So did he. The wind flattened his shirt against his chest. A wild excitement built inside him.

The wind sent tears coursing down Jenny's cheeks, and roared in his ears.

Matt whistled, nudged Master's ribs and took off, this time leaving Jenny in his dust.

Near the quarry, he stopped and turned to watch Jenny ride up. His hungry gaze devoured every plane of her face and traveled the length of her body.

She halted in front of him, a smile on her face, her heavy breathing echoing in the suddenly quiet day, her breasts rising and falling.

Raw desire cramped Matt's gut. Jenny's hat had fallen from her head and hung down her back by the string that crossed her narrow throat. Jesus, did she have to look so much like a...a...a *woman?*

Locks of hair had escaped and hung down the sides of her face. When she reached up to tuck them back into her braid, her high breasts strained against her shirt. Matt was pretty sure she had no idea she was setting a lit match to his tinder-dry loins.

Don't do this to me, Jenny.

Her plaid shirt molded to her breasts and toned arms, tempting Matt to peel if off her and taste the inside of her elbow, or suck on the sensitive skin of her stomach while she squirmed beneath him.

Matt's gut clenched. He dragged his gaze away and gripped Master's reins for all he was worth, ignoring the cramps he set burning in his fingers.

Stop it!

This was insane, ridiculous, history repeating itself, like before when they'd been friends and had ridden and laughed together and entertained the children who'd visited the Sheltering Arms.

Then she had grown up, he'd seen her as a woman instead of his friend and that had ruined everything.

Something inside him broke. It wouldn't happen again. He had to push her away. Fast. He'd work off his debt to Angus and then vamoose. Maybe head up to Canada this time.

What about Jesse?

I don't know.

Because he didn't know, he drew his lips into a mocking smile. His anger at himself found an easy target in Jenny.

"Still crazy after all these years?" he asked. "Running hell-bent over the prairie without a care for anyone else but yourself?"

Jenny's smile vanished. "You were doing it, too."

Good. Keep your distance, woman.

He saw the keen disappointment on her face, especially dark after the exhilaration of their run, but he was trying to stay alive here, trying not to betray Angus.

"Let's find that animal," Jenny said, all business.

Perfect.

She approached the quarry. Matt joined her at the fence that circled it. Sure enough, when he stopped on the rise at the edge of the pit, he spotted a steer on the far side, tangled up in the fence.

"What the heck is that animal doing away from the herd?" Jenny stood on the stirrups and shielded her eyes with her hand.

"He'll have a few scratches on his hide from that barbed wire." Matt stared at the animal. "Good thing Angus is selling him mainly for beef."

"I'll get him out if you want to ride back to the ranch." After the joy of their ride across the prairie, Jenny's coolness hurt, but he'd put it there for a reason.

"Naw," Matt said, "I'll stay and help you get him out."

Jenny nudged Lacey and Matt followed her along the fence to the far side of the pit.

He pulled on his gloves and dismounted. "You have any wire cutters with you?"

Jenny handed him a pair from a small saddlebag.

Matt cut the animal out.

He watched while Jenny led the wild-eyed creature away, soothing the steer's skittishness with whispered words and a firm hand. She'd always had a way with animals and it seemed to have grown even better. He sensed no frustration in her, only the calm patience it took to coax the animal away from the fence.

Matt groaned.

Ah, Jenny, don't make me care for you again.

They returned to the house, slowly leading the steer home. Matt unsaddled both horses while Jenny took the steer to a barn to minister to his torn hide.

Matt finished with the horses then led Masterpiece to a corral to groom him in the sun.

He heard footsteps behind him and turned around.

Jenny was walking toward the stable with Jesse. The kid

didn't look happy. Was she going to make him do chores or something? He seemed pretty young for that.

They disappeared from sight and, full of curiosity, Matt moved Master closer to the open door at the side of the building.

He heard a lot of coaxing coming from Jenny and unhappy whining from Jesse. What was she doing to him?

Matt's curiosity got the better of him and he stepped through the doorway.

Jenny was trying to put her son on a pony, but Jesse folded his legs up like an accordion, refusing to straighten them or separate them over the pony's back.

"Come on, Jesse. Just try it."

"No!" he shouted. "Don't want to."

"I can teach you. It will be fun."

"No, Mom, no!"

Jesse didn't want to learn how to ride a horse? How could a child of Jenny's not love horses? Wait a minute, he was Matt's son, too. How could a kid of *his* not want to ride?

What was Jenny doing wrong?

Jesse struggled to break free of her grasp.

"What's happening?" Matt asked.

"Jesse's going to learn how to ride a horse," she said stubbornly.

"No, I'm not!" Jesse yelled, just as determined.

"Yes, you are," Jenny said. "I mean it, Jesse. We're going to tackle this again."

Jesse wriggled out of her arms and ran from the stable.

Jenny looked as though she was holding on to her patience by the thinnest of ropes.

"Why are you forcing him?" Matt asked. "There has to be a better way to teach him."

He knew immediately that he'd said the wrong thing. A black thundercloud passed over Jenny's face.

"Don't tell me how to handle my son. I've been doing just fine by myself for the past four years."

"Yeah? It's not my fault you had to do it alone, is it?

"Another thing," he said, pointing a finger at her. "I know you thought I'd run off as soon as I found out I had a kid. Well, I haven't."

Now she looked mad enough to spit. "Yet," she said and stormed out.

AFTER LUNCH, Matt headed to the stables.

Angus stepped out of the front door beside Jenny. "Angela needs supplies from town. Will you go?"

"Sure," she said. "Do you have a list?"

"Yup." Angus handed it to her.

Jenny scanned it. "Wow, she needs a lot. Eight bags of triple mix for the garden and a ton of groceries. This will be heavy. I'll get the dolly."

"I can go with you," Matt said. He knew he sounded reluctant, but he could kill two birds with one stone. Help Jenny with her chores and talk to Paula about taking the property off the market. Having a son changed everything, even that.

"I can go alone," Jenny answered tersely.

"There's something I have to do in town." The more he thought about it, the more he wanted to get it done. What if the land was all he had of worth to offer Jesse?

What if Matt didn't have the staying power it would take to be a good father?

At least that land could be his legacy for his son. At least he would have that one thing to give him.

Matt would bulldoze the house, though.

"Okay." Jenny sounded grumpy.

"We can take my truck," he said. She didn't look too happy about riding into town with him.

Too bad.

As they pulled onto the driveway, Matt waved to Angus, but Angus didn't wave back. In fact, he didn't look any happier about Matt going into town with her than Jenny did.

What the heck was that about?

"TOWN HASN'T CHANGED much," Matt murmured as he drove into Ordinary.

Jenny pulled her gaze away from Main Street to study him. His tension was apparent in the stiff way he held himself. He tapped his fingers on the open window well.

She wished she could have left him at the ranch. His shoulders took up more than his fair share of cab space and his heat permeated the air.

Matt stirred, releasing the scent of detergent and dryer sheets from his black shirt.

"Street's busy for midweek," he said.

"How do you feel about coming back?"

"Fine."

"Not nervous? People here used to be pretty hard on you." They'd reacted to his family background, but Matt had pulled his own stunts, too. "This has to be tough."

"Naw."

Jenny glanced at Matt's stony profile. She thought he was lying, but couldn't be sure. She couldn't read him now. One night of sex had changed everything for them. There was a time, though, when she had always known what he was feeling, even when she was a kid.

How did it feel to return to the small town that had ridiculed his father and steered well clear of his crazy mother?

He'd had a lot to prove in this town. And prove it he had—that he was as tough a kid as anyone around.

Jenny had been fascinated by him.

When other kids had mocked him about his family's behavior, he'd get this tight, fake smile and a glassiness to his eyes, but Jenny had always been able to see the vulnerability underneath it.

Why had no one else seen who Matthew Long really was?

Had she seen it only because she knew how he felt about the gossip? No kid wants to be different, to stand out.

After her parents lost the house and then died, Jenny had stood out and hated it. Without warning, she became an orphan, passed for a while from foster home to foster home until she'd grown old enough to work on the Sheltering Arms.

People had been kind, but she'd hated their pity. She just wanted everything to be normal again. She'd lost who she was, and had been working ever since to get herself back.

She'd always known she belonged here, though. Did Matt?

She tried to see the town through his eyes now, but

only saw what she always had—a farming and ranching community town. A bar and a church dished out booze and religion in equal doses. The Legion Hall put on regular dances that everyone attended.

Ordinary wasn't a perfect town, but it sure was a good one.

Matt pulled into a parking spot near the co-op where they'd get the soil, and cut the engine.

The interior of the cab settled into silence.

"You ready for this?" she asked.

He shrugged. "I was already here yesterday."

He was?

When he turned sideways to get out of the truck, his broad shoulders smoothed the wrinkles from the back of his shirt. Jenny hated that she noticed.

She followed him onto the sidewalk.

"We'll get groceries last since Angela wants frozen items. I just have to pick up a couple of things from Scotty's. Wait here. I'll only be a sec."

When the hardware store owner's daughter had acted on a really bad crush on Matt by sleeping with him, Scotty hadn't been impressed. That his sweet little Elsa had lost her virginity to a kid like Matt was a bit too low class for Scotty. Scotty wasn't a bad guy, he'd just had high hopes for his daughter.

When he'd found out Elsa was pregnant, he'd practically hired a lynch mob.

No way did Jenny want Matt in Scotty's store.

The hardware store smelled the same as it had for as far back as Jenny could remember—of sawdust, WD-40 and menthol, the last courtesy of Scotty's addiction to cough drops. She headed to the tools section to pick up a kid-size hammer and a pack of nails with big heads. Jesse had been pestering her for a hammer of his own.

She carried her items to the front counter. "Hey, Scotty. Got a small order today."

"How's things on the Circle K? You busy gearing up for the wedding?"

"Not really. Amy Shelter is taking care of everything for me."

"Uh-huh." Scotty shook his head in a meditative manner while he rang up Jenny's order. "You and Angus. I never would have thought—"

"What do I owe you?" Jenny preemptively handed him a twenty. She didn't want to hear one more person say a word about her marrying Angus. Sure, it seemed weird. The man was thirty-five years older than she was, but they were both good people. They would make it work.

"Is that hammer for Jesse?" Matt's voice behind her startled her. She spun around. Her heartbeat faltered. He was supposed to stay outside.

"For Jesse," she said, keeping her voice even.

"Matt Long, what are you doing back in town?" Scotty asked, his voice as cold as an Alaskan fjord.

"I've got as much right as anyone else to be here."

"Matt, why didn't you wait outside?" Jenny touched his arm. The muscles beneath her fingers were rock hard. She glanced down. His hands were clenched tightly enough to turn the knuckles white.

"I'll be here for a while. I wanted to get this over with."

"You've got a lot of nerve showing up around here after what you did." Scotty's face was red. He raised his fists.

"Whoa, Scotty, calm down," Jenny said. "That was fifteen years ago."

Cripes, were they going to kill each other?

"I haven't forgotten what this animal did to my daughter." Scotty's hostile gaze never left Matt's face.

Matt hadn't defended himself back then and he didn't now.

For God's sake, why not? As angry as Jenny was with Matt, she couldn't let this pass.

"Scotty," she said, building a head of steam, "Elsa was a year older than Matt and ran after him. She was just as responsible as he was."

Scotty stared at her. "What's gotten into you, Jenny? How dare you talk about my daughter like that?"

"It's the truth, Scotty. Elsa is no angel. The whole town knows it. Stop blaming Matt for something that she started."

"Yeah? Well, how about him running away like a yellow dog when he found out she was pregnant? How about leaving her to deal with it all alone?"

There was no defending that.

She risked a glance at Matt.

Matt, facing down a man with a long memory and a deep grudge, kept his expression flat.

"She wasn't alone, Scotty," Jenny said quietly. "She had you and her mother."

Matt, on the other hand, had truly had no one. His parents had never been the kind to rely on.

"Get out of my store. Both of you." The veins in Scotty's neck stood out.

"Oh, Scotty," she said, so disappointed.

She picked up the hammer and nails.

"C'mon, Matt."

She strode to the front door and heard Matt follow her then stop.

Jenny heard him say, "Stay away from my truck."

The bell jangled discordantly over the gentle click Matt closed it with.

"Thanks," he said.

"Yeah." She knew she sounded ungracious, but he'd put her in an awkward spot. She'd made an enemy of Scotty for telling him the truth that no one else had wanted to. As well, she'd just defended a man she didn't want in town either. A man toward whom she wanted no kind thoughts.

"Why did you go in there? You could have easily avoided him until you finished working for Angus."

"Where to now?" Matt asked, closing the subject.

"No. I want answers. After defending you to Scotty, I deserve them."

"I guess I wanted to see if his opinion of me had changed while I was gone." He stared off down the street, hip cocked, one hand in his pocket. "If he'd mellowed."

Not likely.

"What was that about your truck?"

"Scotty stuck a knife or a screwdriver into my tire yesterday."

Jenny sighed. "We need to go to the co-op. For soil for Angela's garden."

They walked along the sidewalk in silence. Matt began whistling softly, a tune she thought she recognized. Disjointed words and phrases ran through her mind until she recognized the song. Dwight Yoakam. "Lonesome Me." Worse still, she remembered a line from the song about the guy thinking himself worthless.

Matt had so much going for him—solid, dependable ranch hand and rodeo star—but what did the people in his hometown remember? His sins.

Jenny's mind shot away from the sympathy for him that flooded through her. *You remember his sins, too.*

She threw the hammer and nails through the open window onto the bench seat of the pickup and headed for the co-op.

She hated this confusion, this feeling of not knowing what to think. Shades of gray bothered her. She liked everything in black and white.

"Come on," she said peevishly. "Let's pick up the rest and go home."

ANGUS NEEDED MOIRA. Worse, his body ached for her. He sped into town, driven to her by all that he'd once had in his life and everything that he now missed. She was key to some of the things he'd lost.

He needed to finish his talk with her.

He had questions and she'd better have answers.

In town, he counted fifty-two steps from his car to the side door of her shop. He wasn't entering through the front door, didn't want to get sidetracked by another encounter with Crusty Christie or any other customers.

Nor did he want to run into Matt and Jenny while they shopped.

Three knocks. Moira. Moira. Moira.

Fifty heartbeats before she answered the door and smiled, before she realized who stood in front of her. The greeting died on her parted lips.

"Angus?" Her wide eyes regarded him steadily, but there was something like excitement underneath the wariness.

It was only the second time he'd seen her this closely since she'd been back in town and she took his breath away.

Three long seconds later, he started to breathe again.

"We need to talk," he said.

She nodded, slowly. "All right. Not here."

He glanced up the stairs behind her, to her apartment above the shop. On the landing at the top of the stairs, a small octagonal window lit a vase of roses sitting on a tiny table.

Curiosity ate at him. Where did she cook? Where did she sit to read a book?

Where did she sleep? No, they couldn't go upstairs. Lord, no. "C'mon. I'm parked in the lane."

Moira hesitated then said, "Just a minute."

He heard her walk down the hall to her store, he assumed to lock the front door and turn the Closed sign around.

She lifted a broad-brimmed straw sun hat and a purse from a hanger on the wall. She stood beside him to lock her door, and he breathed deeply. When she stepped out into the sunlight, he filled his lungs to bursting.

Moira and roses.

He didn't move, letting her back brush his chest and her hair tease his chin. She stared over her shoulder at him, and breathed cinnamon and coffee warmth onto his skin.

If he shifted a fraction of an inch, he could set his lips on the tiny blue vein throbbing at her temple. He held himself rigid.

"Where are we going?" she asked.

"For a drive. I have questions that need answering."

He took her hand in his. She startled, but didn't pull away. It was small and soft in his. His calluses must feel rough to her. He didn't care and held on tight.

With her other hand, she took a pair of sunglasses out of her bag and covered her eyes. Take them off, he wanted to say. It's a crime to hide those gems.

"We shouldn't be meeting," she said, but left her hand in his.

"No. We shouldn't." *I have to.* He opened the passenger door. When she sat, she pulled her skirt around her and drew her bare white legs inside.

Angus sat in the driver's seat and closed the door, turning the car into a one-room asylum for the terminally in love, drenched by the scent of Moira's roses and his own desire. He rolled his window down and started the engine.

Spinning the wheel, he cut through another alley to avoid Main Street and the Crusty Christies of the world.

"Where are you taking me?" Moira asked, her voice soft.

"To a meadow on the back end of my land," he said. "Where we can be private."

She stiffened beside him. "Why do we need privacy?"

He glanced across at her. She held herself still. "I mean to get answers today, Moira."

He rode in silence out of town and along the highway.

At the north end of his property, he turned onto a dirt road and closed his window against the dust. They hit a bump and Angus grabbed Moira's elbow to steady her. On even ground again, he slid his hand down the soft skin of her arm, wove his fingers through hers and held on. Refusing to participate, she kept her fingers straight. They hit another bump and her fingers clung to his.

His thumb took on a mind of its own, caressing the vulnerable stretch of skin between her thumb and forefinger. She shivered. He broadened his strokes, ran his thumb across her wrist. He felt her tremble.

Too soon they arrived in the meadow.

Angus grabbed a denim jacket from the trunk. He set it on the ground under an aspen whose leaves quivered and sparkled in the sun.

Moira stood beside him, twisting the brim of her hat between her fingers.

"Sit," he ordered.

She smiled crookedly. "Yes, master."

He huffed out a laugh. These days he didn't seem to be anybody's master, least of all his own. He barely ran his own ranch, and couldn't control the crazy emotions that plagued him.

Moira sat down beside him and tucked her legs under her skirt.

He reached for her, needed her, like his lungs would collapse if he didn't breathe her in. Now. At this very moment.

With an urgency he hadn't felt since she'd left years ago, Angus pulled her across his lap, threaded his fingers through her hair and kissed her like a man desperate for sustenance.

Yes. This.

He'd been starving. He eased his tongue into her mouth. Drank her in until the gray still life of his days burst into color.

He'd missed her. He'd missed this.

Moira moaned. Her fingers roamed his hair and shoulders with a restlessness that matched his own.

More. He needed more.

He set her back against his up-drawn thighs and found the buttons at the front of her dress.

When his fingers touched her skin, she gasped. Pulled away. Sat up.

While her glazed eyes fought for focus, he fought for air, breathed hard, fanning Moira's disheveled hair around her pale face. Two spots of red appeared high on her cheeks.

"What are we doing?" She shook her head once. "No. I'm not the girl I used to be, Angus. I won't lie down for you so easily."

She was right. He couldn't use her like this when he was committed to someone else.

Nor could he betray Jenny.

What was wrong with him these days? He wasn't an immoral man. He jammed his fingers through his hair.

"I'm sorry." He looked at her over his shoulder.

"I won't do this," she said, her voice firm, her words relentless. "What is it you want from me? An affair?"

He stared at her. God, no.

"I don't know what I want." He held up a hand. "Wait, yeah, I know. I want us to start over. To be twenty-two years old and in love."

He brushed a strand of hair behind her ear. "I want us to have stayed together all this time."

He knew it didn't make sense, but he had to tell her the truth. "I miss Margaret. She was a good person and shouldn't have died so young."

She'd been only thirty.

"I miss my son." He stopped because he couldn't say more without breaking down and sobbing like a baby.

Moira laid a gentle hand on his arm. "I heard. I'm so sorry."

She left her hand there and wrapped her other arm around her knees.

"Tell me about him? What was his name?"

"Kyle." That said it all. Kyle. He'd been unique from the second he was born. The rest of Kyle's story he told with his heart in his throat, finishing with, "He was a great person."

"I wish I'd known him," Moira said and he believed her.

He closed his eyes and sucked in a breath. He had to ask, needed to know.

"Why did you leave if you loved me?" he asked. "No one forced you out of town. We could have had our whole lives together. You could have stayed here and had a good life with me."

"I was young and foolish." She turned to him and the regret in her eyes seared him. "Back then I wanted so much more than this town had to offer."

"I know." He exhaled roughly. "I wasn't good enough for you."

"Yes, you were. I was just afraid you wouldn't be *enough*."

"How was New York?" He couldn't disguise his bitterness. "Was it *enough* for you?"

"No. Not for a long time now." Her shoulders slumped. "A year after I left, I was ready to give up and close the store I opened there and come home. Then I got a big account. It led to other more lucrative accounts. Soon,

I had almost more work than I could keep up with. But I did."

She brushed a fly from her knee. "It was good, for a long while. But lately…I—I've been lonely. When Mother died, I knew it was time to come home."

"You got here too late." Angus leaned closer, lured by Moira's beauty and her sorrow, and by his overwhelming desire to hold her.

The creases on her forehead deepened. "When I heard that you were getting married, I knew I had lost more than I could possibly understand. Why haven't you remarried before now?"

"You know why." His ragged breath stirred a lock of hair curling across her throat.

"Me?" When he nodded, she gripped her hands together in her lap. "Why are you marrying a child?"

His back stiffened. "Jenny isn't a child. She's twenty-seven."

"You're splitting hairs." Her eyes flashed. "She's obscenely young for you and you know it."

She swept her arm across the jacket, sending her hat flying. "Why?" The raw pain in her voice ate at him. "Why marry someone half your age?"

"I need children." The savage whisper torn from his throat nearly killed him. "I want my son back. I want my life back. I want children on the ranch. I need my passion for the land and the work back again."

Moira deflated like a lost balloon.

"Jenny kept the ranch going," he said. "She can give me the rest, too."

Moira dropped her arm. "You're marrying her for children? But you're—"

"Too old?" he asked, harsh and bitter in his middle

age. "Yeah. I know and I don't care." He raised his voice. "I want a family again."

Moira's chest rose and fell in sync with his own. The blood had drained from her face, leaving her ashen.

The violence flooding his veins threatened to choke him.

"I have to go," he choked out and jumped to his feet before he realized where he was and that he had nowhere to go but to take this lovely, aching woman home.

He gripped her elbow and helped her to her feet, his movements slow and steady to rein in all his passion for her and his doubts about his plans. But he was right. He had to marry Jenny. He wanted his life back.

"Angus." He heard the plea in Moira's voice. The face he turned to her was solid, implacable.

"I'm going to do this, Moira." He picked up her hat with careful movements and straightened a dent she'd made in the straw. "I'm going to marry Jenny."

He heard her cry of frustration and walked over to the car.

CHAPTER SIX

ONCE THEY'D FINISHED picking up the groceries for Angela, Matt and Jenny headed home.

They'd been driving awhile when Matt said, "What's that ahead?"

"What the—?" Jenny said.

A distance down the road, a couple of guys stood behind a pickup truck parked on the shoulder. A calf was in the bed, his mouth open like he was lowing.

"Are they— Are they stealing that calf?" Matt asked.

The rustlers saw them approaching. Not bothering to close the tailgate, they ran around the truck, jumped into the front and took off, racing down the road away from them.

"Damn thieves," Jenny cried.

Matt gunned the engine, the truck shot ahead and Jenny fell back against the passenger seat.

"You know those guys?" Matt yelled above the wind whistling through the open windows.

"I can't tell from this distance. I don't think I recognize that truck, though."

Even from this distance, it looked a hell of a lot newer than most vehicles around. Black. No license plate. Matt swerved to avoid a cow running from the field onto the road, trampling what was left of the fence.

"She's after her calf," Jenny said.

"That's Circle K land and a Circle K calf," Matt yelled. "Bastards."

He slammed his hand against the door as they sped down the highway.

At a break in the fence, the pickup spun off the road and hot-tailed it across a field. Matt followed. Jenny grabbed the door handle and held on as they hit the field after the cattle thieves.

As Matt navigated the rough untilled land, the truck bounced around like a toy. They didn't have a hope in hell of catching the jerks.

"Sons of bitches," Matt seethed. "Who are those guys?"

"I wish I knew," Jenny shouted. "I'd shoot them." She braced one hand against the roof.

The pickup truck ahead of them hit a deep hole. The calf flew into the air, bounced out of the truck and landed on the ground feetfirst, hard enough to send a plume of dust into the air.

"No," Jenny moaned.

Matt watched the calf crumple like a hot-air balloon in a windstorm. The pickup shot ahead with a burst of power.

"Stop!" Jenny cried.

"I want to get those guys."

"That calf is hurt."

He slammed on the brakes and the truck fishtailed, but he managed to avoid the calf.

He stopped just shy of the calf, who lay still on the hard-packed earth.

Matt stepped out into the hot dust, cutting a swath

through it with the back of his hand. He knelt beside the still animal and stared at the mangled legs.

"Aw, jeez." He wiped his forehead with his sleeve.

"How bad is he?" Jenny stood behind him with his rifle in her hand. Matt saw the same anger on her flushed face that he felt on his own.

"What a goddamn waste." He stared at the calf and shook his head. "Broken legs."

Behind him, Jenny sucked in air. "Step out of the way, Matt."

He wrapped his fingers around the rifle barrel. "I'll do it."

She stiffened, didn't loosen her grip on the weapon. "It's my job."

"Listen, it's a real shitty thing killing an animal this young." His fingers turned white on the barrel of the gun. "Give me the gun."

She trained her serious eyes on him, unflinching, and said, "That's one of my calves. I'll do it."

The air whistled out between his teeth. He nodded and let go. She was right. It was her job. In the past, he'd never seen Jenny shirk her duties, or shy away from the hard stuff. He didn't remember ever seeing her shoot anything, though.

Jenny pulled the gun away from him.

"Call the ranch and see who can ride out here to fix that fence on the road."

While he pulled his cell phone out of his pocket and punched in the number, Matt watched her chest rise when she filled her lungs, held her breath and sighted down the barrel of the rifle.

The calf lifted his head and sent one pitiful *maa* Jenny's way.

The barrel wavered, then straightened.

The gunshot echoed in the dry sunshine. Startled birds flew out of the trees. A rabbit charged across the field.

It took only the one shot.

Jenny lowered the rifle as if it weighed every one of that calf's three hundred pounds, her face pale.

"You want to sit down for a minute?" Matt touched her elbow.

"I'm fine." She stared at the calf. "This part never gets easy, does it?"

She turned away, hung the rifle back in its holder in the truck's cab and climbed into the driver's seat. She maneuvered the truck around until the back sat a couple of feet away from the calf. Matt jumped into the bed and spread out a blue tarpaulin.

He handed Jenny another tarp that she spread on the ground behind the young animal.

In one brief glimpse, Matt noted sadness on her face, but she got to work, grabbing the broken hind legs of the calf.

They lifted, pushed and pulled the carcass onto the tarpaulin. Jenny grunted, low in her throat. After they finally managed to wrestle it onto the back of the truck, he closed and locked the tailgate.

Jenny stood beside him, panting, sweat beading on the freckles across her nose and cheeks.

Damn, she was strong.

Damned if he didn't want to take her in his arms to comfort her. She wasn't okay, but neither was she falling apart. She was just getting the job done as well as he or Angus would have. He felt something rise in his chest, something soft, and realized it was pride. He tried to shake it off—she wasn't his—but he couldn't.

He wanted to reach for her, not for comfort now, but for one hell of a kiss to show her how proud he was. He shoved his hands into his back pockets.

Matt stared at her, but her gaze never wavered.

"Get in." Her tone held a trace of flint.

He tapped her door, then ran around the truck and jumped in.

They found six pairs of cows and calves wandering the road, including the calf's mother. A hundred other pairs grazed contentedly in the pasture.

"This'll be hard on her," Jenny said as she stepped out of the truck. "That calf's twin died at birth. She's alone now."

She whistled and shouted, "Go on, back into the field," herding them on one side while Matt controlled the other, until the cows were back where they belonged.

Matt straightened the fence as best he could. "They can still get out, but they won't. Not as long as the fence looks sturdy." He turned to her with a grin, needing to make her feel better, but her answering smile was pained.

"Do you mind taking the groceries back to the ranch?" She looked away from him and raised a hand to shade her eyes, studying the sun-drenched field.

"Where are you going?" he asked.

"I'm going to walk across the fields. Make sure the cows are all right. I'll be okay."

"Sure. Do the Eriksons still take dead cattle?"

"Yeah. Cam pays good money. Can you get the calf there?"

"Will do. See you at the ranch."

He watched her start her walk home. In the distance, a couple of men rode four-wheelers toward her. Will and Hip, maybe. They'd take care of fixing that fence properly.

Matt drove over to the Eriksons' and left the carcass there. Cam wrote a check to Angus for the meat.

Once at the ranch, Matt backed the truck up to the door of the stable to rinse it out with the hose. He sprayed the bed and the tarpaulin until every trace of blood was gone. He washed the dirty red water away from the yard and into a field. He threw the rag he'd used into the garbage then leaned against the big utility sink inside the stable, his fingers gripping the edge.

THE SUN BEAT DOWN on Jenny's back, overheating her through her plaid shirt. Her eyes felt as if they had a sandbox full of grit in them.

Still, she trudged up the hill, trying to get emotional fallout from the incident out of her system so she wouldn't cry in front of the men. Why was she so weak?

Living in a man's world was tough. She had to work twice as hard to measure up. She knew any number of the ranch hands would have found that difficult, but none would have shed a tear. She didn't want to, she wouldn't, but her chest hurt from the strain of holding sobs in.

Give yourself a break, Jen, you just shot a calf while he stared up at you with trust in his eyes.

Oh, God, those eyes. Maybe I should have tried—

There was nothing you could do. The animal had four broken legs. You saw a lot of pain in those eyes, too.

The argument went around and around in her mind during the walk home.

When she reached the top of the rise that overlooked the ranch house, she sat down heavily. A long shaky breath escaped her.

She plucked a blade of grass and tore it apart.

Soon, very soon, she would see all her dreams realized.

The day Dad had declared bankruptcy, she'd thought those dreams had died—of her children running across this land, of a husband she would love passionately, of annual barbecues with friends and family gathered around, of sunset rides with her husband and children and surveying the fields they'd tilled and planted themselves, watching their cattle grow big and healthy like their children, reaping the rewards of hard work.

After they'd lost the ranch, her family had gone to live in town. Six months later, her parents were in a car accident and her mother had been killed. Her dad survived his injuries but went into a decline that took his life a year later.

After that, the girl who'd known her place on earth, whose connection to her home and land had been profound, had become an unwilling nomad.

The first foster home hadn't been anywhere near Ordinary. She'd fought that first home hard and had kept fighting until subsequent homes had brought her closer and closer to town. She didn't stop until she was old enough to work on the Sheltering Arms.

A sigh so deep it seemed to start in the soles of her feet escaped her.

C'mon, Jen, time to go home. You did all right today.

She needed to see Jesse, to be with her son. His sweetness and high spirits never failed to lift her own. She hadn't planned to be a single mom, but she was doing her best to love him enough for two parents.

Angus helped. Soon, for all intents and purposes, he would be Jesse's father.

Matt wouldn't stay. Sure, she'd defended him in town, but she knew better than to expect much from him. Certainly not as a parent.

She stood to walk down the hill for dinner.

A cloud passed over the sun. Jenny saw rain on the horizon.

"WHATCHA DOIN'?"

Matt turned from brushing Master toward the small voice behind him. Jesse stood on the third rail on the outside of the corral fence, hanging from the top railing by his armpits. He banged his palms on the inside of the fence, trying to get Master's attention.

Matt watched him as though he was some kind of alien. Matt had dealt with a lot of children the years he'd worked at the Sheltering Arms and had never felt like this—tongue-tied and inadequate.

"Doesn't that hurt your underarms?" Matt pointed his chin toward the kid.

"Nope," Jesse chirped. "I do it all the time."

"What're you doing here?" Matt brought the brush down on Master's dark back. The horse preened under the rasp of bristles across his hide. "Don't you have school or something?"

"I'm too young for school." The boy looked at Matt as if he had a horseshoe for a brain. Where this kid was concerned, he probably did.

Where he'd been easy with the children on the Sheltering Arms, enjoying their antics, he was afraid of saying or doing something wrong with this one.

"What's your horse's name?" the boy asked.

"Masterpiece."

The kid bobbed on his feet, onto his toes, then down on his heels. Up. Down. Up. Down.

"You're going to ruin the heels of those boots if you're not careful." Did he just sound like a father? Weird.

"I do this all the time. My mom lets me."

"Yeah?" He couldn't help it, had to ask, "You like your mom?" Matt felt sneaky for asking, but he was curious. He'd seen signs of maturity in her. Were they real?

"Uh-huh."

"What's she like?"

"Nice. She lets me go to Hank's all the time." He climbed up to the second railing, placed his hands on the top one and lifted his feet away from the fence, balancing himself on his palms. "She let me keep a frog I found."

"That right? A frog?"

"His name's Bucket."

Matt smothered a laugh. "Where'd he get a name like Bucket?"

Jesse tilted his head. "I brought him home in a bucket."

He climbed to the top railing and sat facing Matt, hooking his boot heels onto the second railing. "I got a fish, too."

Matt turned to him and said, "Yeah? What's his name? Bowl? Tank?" but the boy wasn't listening. He was staring at Matt's belt buckle with his mouth wide open.

"What did you get that for, mister?"

"Rodeo." Matt returned to grooming his horse.

"I'm gonna rodeo when I grow up. Can you teach me how, mister?"

Matt wasn't a mister, he was a father, but Jesse wasn't allowed to know that.

Jenny probably wouldn't want him to teach the boy anything, to get that close to him. Maybe he should to spite her. She should have told him about his son.

What would you have done about it? If you're this awkward with him as a four-year-old, how would you have felt holding him as an infant?

Matt set the brush on the top railing beside Jesse. Up close, the deep blue of the boy's eyes were shot through with small flecks of golden honey, like the warm yellow flecks in Jenny's eyes. First likeness to Jenny Matt recognized in the boy aside from the freckles.

He stared, having trouble taking in that this tyke was a mixture of him and Jenny, that Jesse was the result of that one night.

"Watch!" the boy said then twisted himself onto his abdomen on the top railing, sticking his arms and legs straight out, balancing on nothing but his flat little stomach.

"Hey," Matt yelled and grabbed him under the arms, hauling him up and setting him on his feet outside the corral. "You're too old to be doing something that dumb."

His pulse was racing. Damn. The kid had the same streak of recklessness Jenny used to have. It was in the genes.

Jesse got a stubborn look and tilted his head. "What's so dumb about it?"

"You could fall off and crack your head open."

"No, I won't. I like doing it. It's fun."

"Too bad."

"I can do it if I want to."

"Not while I'm around you can't."

"You're mean." Jesse stamped his foot and ran off. "I don't like you, mister."

Wow, those words had never hurt so much. Some of the kids at Hank's had been sour and reeling from the unlucky shit life had dealt them in the form of cancer and, most times, poverty. He'd been called plenty of things before they learned to settle in and have fun.

It had never bothered him then, but it sure did now coming from Jesse.

"Yeah, well, tough," Matt called to Jesse's retreating back.

Mature, Long. Real mature.

He saw Jenny standing near the house. Crap. She'd heard him.

She stormed toward him like a mother lion with claws bared. "What did you say to Jesse?"

"I told him he couldn't balance on his stomach on top of the fence or he'd fall off and break his skull open," Matt retorted. He'd been right to stop the kid, dammit.

"Oh," Jenny said, and the starch left her spine. "Okay, thanks. That's good."

Later that day, he saw Jenny trying to force Jesse to ride and Jesse resisting. Again.

Leave it alone. It's none of your business.

Jenny had made that clear.

He's your child, too.

As Jesse ran from the barn crying, Matt thought, *Yeah, I understand what you're going through, kid.*

Matt entered the stable.

JENNY PRESSED her forehead against Flora's hide and bit her tongue. She'd tried to get Jesse to ride again only to have it end in tears—again.

They lived in ranching country and always would. It was unthinkable that a boy would grow up on a ranch and not learn how to ride, but she'd run out of patience.

She'd been at this for a year, bashing her head against the wall of Jesse's resistance. She couldn't do it much longer.

"Why doesn't he want to ride?"

Jenny heard Matt's voice behind her and closed her eyes. Did he always have to hear her failing with Jesse? What about all the times they had fun together, all the times he was warm and sweet and fun instead of recalcitrant?

"A kid of yours should have been born in the saddle," Matt said. "He looks fearless on that jungle gym in the backyard."

"He is," she agreed. As much as she still wanted to limit his exposure to Jesse, she might as well just tell him. Maybe he'd think her less of a failure as a mother if he understood. "The first time he got up on the pony, he was only three, but he loved it."

"What happened?"

"A storm blew in. Before the rain hit, I was leading Jesse into the stable when a crack of thunder came out of nowhere."

Jenny lifted the pony's saddle from her back. Jesse wouldn't be riding today. "It startled a mouse out of a pile of straw, who scooted under Flora's hooves and spooked her. She reared and tossed Jesse on the ground."

A quirky lift of one corner of Matt's mouth had her asking, "What?"

"Flora?"

She smiled. "Yes, *Flora.*"

Matt turned serious again. "Too many things happened together, I guess."

Jenny nodded. "Exactly. Now Jesse's afraid of horses and thunder."

"Can I try?" Matt asked.

No freaking way. "No."

"Why not? He's my child, too."

She took a brush and started in on grooming Flora. "I won't have you making friends with him and then running off."

"I'm going to whether you like it or not."

"Run off?" she snapped sarcastically. It was a good thing Flora liked to be brushed hard. "Yeah, I know."

Matt flushed. "I meant that I would get to know him, not that I'd leave."

Jenny stopped brushing and said quietly, "But you will do that, too."

She knew he couldn't deny it. She watched him try

to come up with the right words, but they both knew Matt wasn't a guarantee-giving kind of guy.

She wanted guarantees for her child. Angus was a man who could give her those and never back out of them.

Matt's lips twisted and he stared out the door to where Jesse was sitting in the sunlight with his arms and legs crossed and his bottom lip sticking out. "All right, listen. I had the same problem with horses when I was little."

Matt? "You did? I find that hard to believe."

"Yeah. You'd never know it now. I came to like horses."

"Like" was an understatement. She thought of the joy on his face when he'd ridden past her during their impromptu race yesterday. It had been stunning what that joy had done to her, stirring long-forgotten feelings. They used to have so much fun racing.

It also stirred the urges she'd developed toward him in adolescence.

He'd ruined it minutes later with his insult, though. Thank God. She had no right nurturing those kinds of feelings for Matt.

"Can you remember why you were afraid?"

"My dad. He shoved me on his own horse too early. Dad didn't believe in starting small on ponies. The guy was all about trial by fire."

"How did you get over it?"

"Funny thing. Dad put that fear there, and then forced it out of me. Made me ride every day, rain or shine, fear or not. One day, I finally saw the light when the horse took off across a flat field and wouldn't stop. Somewhere on that ride, the pleasure took hold."

"I'll only use so much force on Jesse," Jenny said. "Then I'll quit." She walked away.

MATT SWORE up and down that he would get to know Jesse whether the boy liked him or not, whether Matt knew how to deal with him or not. He was finished work for the day and found Jesse, in the kitchen with Angela.

"Angela," Matt said. "Is it okay if I take Jesse outside?"

"Sure. He'd like that." Angela smiled. "Jenny won't be back for an hour."

Matt turned to Jesse. "Do you want to learn how to rope a calf?"

"Yeah!" Jesse jumped up from the table where he'd been cutting cookies out of raw dough for the house-keeper. He ran for the door.

"Just a minute." Matt stopped him with a hand on his shoulder. "Wash your hands first."

"I don't got to."

"Have to," Matt corrected.

"No, I don't."

"C'mon, kid." Matt steered him down the hall to the powder room and squirted soap into his hands. "Now, wash."

When he realized Matt was serious, Jesse did what he was told. Matt remembered how the guest kids on the Sheltering Arms had tested limits. Seemed that kind of thing was universal.

Now that he knew he couldn't push Matt around, Jesse was fine. Matt laughed to himself. How long would it last? An hour?

As it turned out, it lasted half that long.

There wasn't a single kid-size rope on the ranch. Jesse wore out real quick trying to use a full-size rope, leaving them both irritated and on edge.

Finally, Matt said, "That's enough for today."

Jesse ran for the house and Matt strode to the bunkhouse and flopped onto his bed.

How was he supposed to get to know his son when they had so much trouble connecting and Matt didn't have a clue why?

He'd *never* had this problem with kids before.

Matt punched his pillow.

He refused to quit.

CHAPTER SEVEN

THE THIRD TIME Matt witnessed Jenny try to get Jesse on a horse, he'd had enough.

She walked from the stable carefully, like someone who was trying to hold on to her temper really hard, leaving Jesse to sulk in a corner.

Enough was enough. That kid had it in him to ride.

By hook or crook, whether Jesse and he got along today or not, Matt was going to teach his son how to ride.

Jenny doesn't want you involved. Too bad. The kid was his, too.

He approached Jesse, leading Flora down the aisle, and squatted in front of him.

"Hey," he said.

"Hey," Jesse mumbled, picking at a scab on his elbow.

"Don't you like horses?"

"I like 'em. I don't want to ride 'em."

"I know what part of the problem is."

Jesse's head popped up. "You do?"

"Sure. It's your pony's name."

"Really?"

"Sure. How can any pony be happy with a name like Flora? It's too old-fashioned and flowery." What a load of crap. That made no sense at all, but Matt didn't know what else to say.

"It is?"

"Yup. We need to rename her. Give her a sense of pride so she won't go tossing kids on their butts. What would be a good name?"

"Buttercup?" Matt almost laughed out loud—another flower name—but Jesse was dead serious. "I got a book. The horse is named Buttercup."

"You like that book?"

Jesse nodded so hard a lock of hair fell onto his forehead. "A lot! Buttercup wears a hat with holes cut out for her ears and she really likes it."

"There's an idea. Maybe if we make Flora—I mean, Buttercup, happier, it'll be easier to ride her. Let's go."

"Where to?"

"To find a hat we can use."

Matt turned and walked away, not giving Jesse a chance to resist. He left Flora in the corral and walked through the gate without looking back. A second later, the boy followed.

Curiosity had won out.

In the bunkhouse, Matt found an ancient brown cowboy hat on a hook and hoped like hell it wasn't somebody's treasure, because he was about to give it to a horse.

Jesse followed him back to the corral, taking Matt's hand along the way. Matt looked down. Jesse's hand looked incredibly small in his, felt impossibly tiny. He couldn't believe his own had ever been that small.

Matt held the hat up to Flora's head and eyeballed the distance between her ears.

He pulled a multi-tool out of his pocket and used the knife to cut into the hat.

"Let me see," Jesse cried.

Matt squatted and Jesse put one hand on his sleeve. Matt felt the heat of it through his shirt and it warmed more than just his skin. That heat traveled through his veins to lodge in his heart for good.

Fruit of my loins. Shit, how corny was that? But Matt couldn't get over that this little guy had started as a seed too small for the eye to see. Molded in Matt's own image.

No, kid, don't become me. Become a better man than me.

What had Jenny said about Angus?

He's the better man.

She might as well have ripped Matt's heart from his chest, but he couldn't deny the truth. Angus was the better man.

But Jesse was *Matt's* son.

Whether Matt could bring himself to stay or not, this was a forever moment. He swallowed hard. Not one thing in his life had ever felt as good as his son's touch.

Jesse left his hand there and watched patiently as Matt finished cutting two holes for ears.

He stood to place it on the pony's head then thought better of it. Instead, he scooped Jesse up into his arms and gave him the hat.

Jesse set it on Flora's head. Matt helped to push her ears through.

"There you go, Buttercup," Jesse said.

Flora shied away and tried to shake off the hat.

Jesse's lower lip jutted out. "She doesn't like it."

"Wait," Matt said. He stroked Flora's nose and crooned to her. "Beautiful girl. Aren't you pretty?"

He felt Jesse staring at him and explained, "That's how you talk to horses when you want them to do something. Try it."

Jesse stuck out his hand and touched Flora's nose. "Pretty girl," he mimicked.

Still Flora tried to shake off the hat.

Matt pulled a caramel out of his pocket. He unwrapped it and handed it to Jesse. "Here. Try this."

Jesse held the candy out and Flora sniffed it. When she lifted it eagerly from Jesse's palm, the boy giggled.

"That tickles. Look! She likes it."

As she rolled the treat on her tongue, Flora settled down and stopped fighting the hat. She butted Matt's breast pocket looking for another caramel.

Jesse laughed.

"Tell her she can have another one after she gives you a ride."

Again, Jesse mimicked Matt's earlier crooning and repeated his words.

"Okay. Let's get you up on Flora's back."

"She's Buttercup!"

"Right. Buttercup. Listen, that's a mouthful. Can we call her Butter? Like a nickname?"

"'Kay. That's a good name."

Matt lifted him, but Jesse pulled up his legs. "Hey," Matt said, "I'm not going to let go."

"Honest?" Jesse whispered.

"Honest."

Jesse lowered his legs and settled into the small saddle.

Matt wrapped his arm around Jesse's waist and Jesse placed his arm across Matt's shoulders. It didn't quite reach his far shoulder and was light across Matt's back.

They walked around the corral like that, countless times, until Matt felt Jesse's resistance start to give way, felt him relax and enjoy the ride.

He stared at the smile on Jesse's face. Who would have thought walking in circles beside his son on a horse could bring Matt so much pleasure?

"Can I ride by myself now?"

"You sure you want to?"

Jesse nodded.

Matt taught him how to hold the reins properly and how to control his horse.

With Jesse's expression a mixture of fear and excitement, Matt let go. Jesse continued his circuits around the corral with a big grin on his face.

The sense of pride Matt felt nearly knocked him off his feet. In the vastness of the world, Jesse had just accomplished a small feat, but for Jesse it was huge—*huge*—and Matt couldn't hold back his own grin.

Man, his eyes felt damp. How crazy was that? Dad had beaten into him that a man never cries, but at this moment, Matt didn't give a damn.

He wanted to teach Jesse more things, and give him stuff, the kinds of toys he'd always wanted as a child. Not all the new electronic gadgetry like iPods and computers that kids had these days, but simple tools like compasses and binoculars and maybe a telescope.

Hey, a bow and a quiver of arrows would be great. Matt could teach Jesse how to shoot at a target.

Did Angus still have his iron horseshoes? They would

probably be too heavy for Jesse to lift. He might be able to toss quoits, though.

Matt's brain wouldn't quit.

JENNY CLOSED HER EYES and leaned her forehead on the living room windowpane.

She'd just watched Matt do what she hadn't been able to do with Jesse in the past year. How? By putting a hat on the pony? What was that about?

Jenny pounded her head a couple of times against the glass. She didn't want this happening.

This was exactly what she had been afraid of.

Jesse was falling for his dad, so much faster than Jenny could have predicted. Maybe she should pack a bag for herself and Jesse and go away until her wedding day, pull one of Matt's own tricks on him. Run away.

That would be cruel, though, to Matt and probably to Jesse.

Angus entered the room. "What are you doing?"

Jenny lifted her face away from the glass. "Matt just taught Jesse how to ride Flora."

"Really? How'd he manage that when the rest of us couldn't?"

"I don't know, but it has something to do with putting a cowboy hat on Flora."

"What?"

"Look."

Angus stood beside her and she leaned into his warmth.

"I'll be damned," Angus said.

"I'm scared," Jenny whispered. She looked up into his sympathetic face. "They're bonding, Angus. What happens when he leaves?"

Angus stared out the window, not appearing to be totally happy.

"How do you feel about Matt getting to know his son?" she asked. He was involved in this, too. Angus was expecting to be Jesse's dad after they got married.

"It's good. It's the way it should be."

"Oh, Angus, you're always so fair. Doesn't it worry you that Matt might replace you in Jesse's heart?"

Angus didn't answer for a while then said, speaking low, "Maybe."

ANGUS DIDN'T KNOW what to feel. He watched two generations out there—Matt, his surrogate son, and Jesse, his almost son—and missed Kyle and the chance to have his own grandchildren. He could have more children with Jenny and raise brothers and sisters for Jesse, and then have grandchildren many years from now.

But Matt. Where would he fit in?

Angus strode from the house and walked to his car. He needed to sort out his feelings.

When Matt saw him, he called Angus over to the fence, his face alight with the kind of excitement he'd never seen there when Matt was younger.

"Are you heading into town?" Matt asked.

Angus nodded. He couldn't speak to Matt right now, not until he figured out what was wrong, why he couldn't be happy for Matt.

Pulling a hundred bucks out of his wallet, Matt handed it to Angus. It looked as if that cleaned him out. "Can you pick up a pair of binoculars for Jesse? If you can't find any in Ordinary, can you get me a compass instead?"

Angus silently tucked the money into his pocket.

"Hey," Matt said. "Do you still have that telescope of Kyle's?"

Angus nodded.

"Can I borrow it tonight?"

"Sure. It's in Kyle's closet. Help yourself."

He had no intention of going in there and hunting it out for Matt. Angus hadn't entered Kyle's room since his death.

He got into his car, anxious to get away from the heartwarming scene of the burgeoning relationship between Matt and Jesse. Even the reasonable thought that Matt deserved it did nothing to allay Angus's new irrational jealousy.

JENNY AND MATT STARTED cleaning the pile of trash that had accumulated on the far side of the barn beside the workshop door—bald tires, lengths of rusted wire, part of a stove, a dented truck fender and the list went on. It would take more than one afternoon to clear it out.

Since both of the ranch's trucks were out, they tossed the refuse into Matt's pickup to haul to the dump.

The entire time, Jesse followed Matt, imitating everything he did. Matt had already outfitted the boy with a too-big pair of work gloves like his own. When he'd pushed Jesse's tiny hands into them, it had just about melted his heart.

This was good. Too good.

By dinnertime, the truck bed was full to overflowing and they'd made decent progress on the pile. Jesse insisted on following Matt to the bunkhouse while he washed up and changed into clean clothes for dinner.

Matt walked to the house with his hand on Jesse's

small shoulder, then, like a real father, sent him upstairs to change and wash his hands.

Later Matt followed Jenny into the kitchen with Kyle's old telescope in his hand.

"I know he would love it," he said. "What kid wouldn't?"

Jenny rinsed the glass she'd been using and set it in the sink. Jesse had hung around with Matt for the rest of the afternoon and evening, following him like a truncated shadow. Now Matt wanted to take him out past his bedtime to lie in the grass and look at the stars.

Things were moving too quickly.

"He's still young. I keep him to a schedule."

"So what? He can break it for one night."

Jenny spun to face him. "Listen, I've been his mother for four years. I know what he needs and what he can do without for a while."

Matt pushed one hand into his pocket and stared at her. "I missed those four years. I want to make up for them now."

Jenny knew she'd robbed him and guilt ate away at her, gnawed its way through her stomach lining. That he'd spoken the words quietly instead of in anger made her feel even worse.

"Okay," she said. "But only for tonight. Tomorrow he goes to bed at his regular time."

"Sure," Matt said too lightly.

"Promise?"

"Promise."

Jenny wondered how much Matt Long's promises were worth these days.

"I'll get you a couple of blankets."

"Blankets? It's May."

"Exactly. The evenings are still cool and Jesse will get cold lying on the ground."

"Fine. Whatever. Can we just get them and go?"

Matt was behaving like an eager boy. This parenting business was all new to him. What would happen when the novelty wore off? What would happen when he had to be a real parent, to use discipline when Jesse acted up, or nurse him when he got sick? When he had to do the work and not just the play?

Now he was having fun. What about when that fun stopped? What then, Matthew Long?

UPSTAIRS, MATT TOOK the pair of heavy blankets that Jenny handed him, then ran downstairs to tell Jesse what they were going to do.

Jesse squealed and ran for the back door.

Jenny ran to Kyle's old bedroom at the rear of the house and opened the window in time to hear Jesse say outside in the yard, "Here, Matt, here's a good spot."

Compelled to watch everything that Matt did with her son, she left the lights off so there would be no reflections on the glass. So she wouldn't miss anything.

Matt spread the blankets and lay down on them. Jesse lay down beside him, tucking his small hip against Matt's side.

Don't, Jenny thought, *don't get close to him.*

Matt put his arm under Jesse's head and adjusted the telescope for him. He held it while Jesse looked through the lens.

"Wow, look! The moon is real big."

"See all the stars?"

Jesse grabbed the telescope and moved it around wildly.

"Whoa," Matt said, taking it back. "Let me find some for you."

He pointed straight up. "Know what those stars are?"

"What?" Jesse asked.

"The Milky Way." Matt focused the telescope, then handed it back to Jesse, holding it steady.

"Can you see stars now?"

"Yeah, but they just look like lights. They don't look like the pointy stars on the Christmas tree."

"No, they don't, do they?"

"Show me more, Matt."

Jenny watched Matt show her son more stars. She wished she was down there with them, but she hadn't been invited, and her guilt had prevented her from asking. She wanted to lie on her son's other side, tuck him against her body instead of Matt's, keep him safe in the world she'd created for him and planned to cement with her marriage to Angus.

She heard Matt say, "I'll teach you about all of the stars."

No! Jenny's blood surged through her veins. She barely held herself back from leaning out the window and yelling at Matt to stop making promises he probably wouldn't keep.

A few minutes later Matt took the telescope from Jesse. Even from up here, Jenny could tell that he'd fallen asleep.

Matt watched him sleep, stared at Jesse's small head tucked against his shoulder. In the light spilling from the kitchen window, Jenny saw Matt touch Jesse's hair, run it through his fingers with reverence.

He stayed there for a long time, watching his son sleep.

Jenny remained at her post at the window, watching a quiet scene that nearly broke her heart. This was the way it should have been all along.

Eventually, Matt picked up Jesse and brought him inside.

Jenny ran to the top of the stairs and waited.

Matt appeared at the bottom with Jesse curled in his arms like a trusting little puppy. When he reached the top Jenny reached out to take him, but Matt shook his head.

"Show me his room."

No. He's mine.

Jenny led the way to the front of the house and opened a door. She'd painted his room light blue and his furniture every color of the rainbow. Matt laid him on the bed and Jenny moved to take off his clothes, but Matt brushed her aside.

"I'll do it."

That's my job. "I'll get his pajamas."

"No, I will. I want to know where his stuff is."

Jenny pointed to the top drawer of his dresser.

Matt undressed their son and looked around for a laundry basket. Jenny gestured to the plastic bucket sitting below the fake basketball net she'd hung on the back of his door. Usually, Jesse threw his clothes through the net and, when he got lucky and actually got one in, it dropped through into the laundry bucket.

Matt smiled and tossed the clothes into the bucket.

He dressed Jesse's tiny body in the pajamas then tucked him under his blankets.

When he leaned over and kissed his forehead, the

scene was so sweetly tender that Jenny didn't know whether she wanted to kiss Matt or give him a boot in the rear end.

Those were all *her* jobs, not his. Jesse was *her* son. But that was unfair. He was Matt's son, too.

Jenny turned on a small night-light and closed the door behind them, leaving a gap in case he needed her during the night.

"He didn't brush his teeth." Her tone was faintly censorious.

"Does he brush them every night? And every morning? Is he pretty good at doing it, or do you have to get on his case about it?"

He'd been pestering her with questions all evening and she was tired of it.

"Matt, I'm heading to bed."

She walked down the hall to her room. Just before closing the door, she caught him watching her. He looked…lost.

She hardened her heart and tried not to feel sorry for him. She had her own unruly emotions to sort through.

IN THE DAYS that followed, Jesse trailed Matt everywhere. Jenny felt as though she'd lost her son, or at least had lost some of her control over him.

Jenny had to force him to stay with Angela for a few hours every day so she and Matt could get work done.

They finished clearing out the junk pile and Matt took three loads to the dump.

They delivered salt blocks to the bulls, who craved it and thundered over. This, plus the minerals laid out by the crew all winter, would keep the cattle healthy.

They oiled and greased all of the ranch equipment, including two big Caterpillars used to shovel manure, earth or snow, depending on the weather.

One morning they took over driving out to the fields to feed the cattle while the crew started early on the fencing that needed to be finished.

As ranch foreman, Jenny spent hours on solitary rides on horseback or in a truck, checking up on the crew and the land, and trying to anticipate problems. It was strange to have Matt around so much and it left her feeling distracted and confused.

Angus became broody and spent more time away from the house, sometimes riding his land and sometimes in town, she guessed. She didn't know for sure. Jenny worried about him, and wondered what was going on in his head.

One night, Matt wanted to take Jesse to sleep in the bunkhouse with him.

Jenny fought it, but Jesse begged her to let him and, along with Matt's pressure, it was more than she could resist.

"Okay," she finally said. "I'll pack him a bag."

"Pack him a bag?" Matt's tone was incredulous. "We're only going to the bunkhouse on the other side of the barn."

"I know, but routine is important to children his age. He needs his toothbrush and his bedtime story."

To Jesse, she said, "Go pick one of your books for Matt to read to you before bed."

While Jesse chose a book, rummaging on his bookshelves until he found the one he wanted, she packed a toothbrush, toothpaste, his pajamas and a bathrobe in case he got cold during the night.

"Hey, Matt," Jesse hollered downstairs, "I'm bringing Buttercup's story. 'Kay?"

"Sounds good," Matt called up.

So that was where he'd gotten the new name for Flora. Butter. Part of Buttercup. And the hat. Jenny had forgotten all about that book.

Jesse ran down ahead of her. "I think I packed everything he'll need," she said.

Matt smoothed a frown from her forehead. "Stop worrying."

It was the first time he'd touched her deliberately since he'd come back, and the scrape of his callus felt good. She shivered and pulled away from him, too abruptly, judging by his frown, but she couldn't worry about his feelings. She needed to keep her distance.

"I'm not worried."

"Liar." Matt grinned. He and Jesse were the only two who seemed cheerful these days.

They left the house and Jenny felt lost. Angus was out somewhere again. Her footsteps rang hollow on the hardwood floors.

She turned on the TV, flipped through the channels and switched it back off. Nothing but junk.

She ran a scented bubble bath and tried to read a romance novel. That lasted half an hour.

After she dried off and spread her favorite cream on her skin, she pampered herself with a manicure and pedicure, a rarity. Hank's wife, Amy, had taught her how to take care of her nails properly, but most of the time, this stuff was a luxury.

Finally, all out of things to do, she climbed into bed and turned off the light.

Sleep refused to come.

ANGUS SAT IN HIS CAR across the road from Moira's shop, thinking about what-ifs and should-have-beens.

He watched a shadow he knew to be Moira cross in front of the window above the shop in the only room with a lamp burning. She lived up there. Had when she was young, with her mother.

He'd wanted to try again to talk to her about his crazy, jumbled feelings, but realized as soon as he'd arrived that meeting her up there, in her apartment, would be an enormous mistake.

A warm light shone in the room, filtered through the closed curtains. So she still used the same bedroom she had when she was young.

The light went out.

He tucked his palms under his thighs and listened to the gentle patter of rain on the roof of the car, staring at a dark window that matched the emptiness in his heart.

Moira.

MATT HAD BEEN TRYING for over an hour to get Jesse settled down in the bed beside his, but the other ranch hands were playing cards at the far end of the bunkhouse. He'd already told them Jesse was his son. They'd taken it in stride.

Jesse's head shot up at every remark, every question, every game won or lost.

Jenny had been right. This was a terrible idea. Still, in for a penny...

He read *Buttercup's Favorite Hat* for the tenth time, then turned off the light for the tenth time. The only other lights on were over by the card game, and for

Jesse's sake, the boys had turned on just enough to see their hands.

Matt tucked the covers around Jesse and kissed his clean, soap-scented forehead. For the tenth time.

"Now, stay put and go to sleep."

Matt lay down in the semidarkness and stared at the ceiling.

"Matt?" Jesse said. He sounded sleepy. At last.

"Yeah?"

"I love you."

My God. Dear God. Matt had had no idea how this would feel, to hear his child's sweet high voice murmur that he loved his dad. And Matt was that dad, even if Jesse didn't know it yet.

Matt drifted off to sleep on a high.

He was awakened by a massive crack of thunder and Jesse screaming, "Mommy! Mommy!"

"You okay?" one of the ranch hands mumbled to Jesse.

"I got him," Matt answered. He picked up Jesse, hugged him and rubbed his back. "Hey, it's okay, partner. It's just a little thunder."

"It's dark in here." Uncertainty and tears shook Jesse's voice.

"Yeah, that's how the ranch hands like to sleep."

"I want my mo-o-om," Jesse said, sobbing.

"You sure? She's probably asleep."

"I want her."

He sounded so miserable, Matt couldn't deny him. Maybe if Matt could get Jesse to sleep in his own bed, he wouldn't awaken Jenny.

"Something smells stinky in here," Jesse said, calmer now that he knew he'd see his mom.

"One of the guys farted."

"Mine don't smell like that."

"You weren't drinking beer tonight."

"Beer makes farts stinky?"

"It's been known to."

"I'm never gonna drink beer in my whole life."

"Want to bet?"

Matt heard someone chuckle, then roll over.

He pulled Jesse's robe on over his pajamas, slipped his own boots on and covered both their heads with a raincoat from beside the door.

Then he ran out into the night. Rain pounded on the coat as they crossed the yard.

Matt entered the house just as a furry pink thing threw herself at him and Jesse.

Jenny.

"What's wrong?" she cried. "Jesse, are you okay? What happened?"

"Nothing serious," Matt answered. "Thunder woke him."

Jenny grabbed Jesse and squeezed him.

Matt shook the rain off the coat and hung it on a hook by the door.

"Mom," Jesse said, but it came out muffled since Jenny had his face crushed against her chest. Her soft, braless chest. Her very nice chest.

"I can't breathe," Jesse said, and Jenny eased her grip. Cripes, you'd think she'd never had the kid out of her sight before. Did she always worry when Jesse was away from her? Or only when Jesse was with him?

"How'd you know we were coming over here?" Matt asked.

"I heard the bunkhouse door close."

"Really? Over the thunder and the rain?" Mother's ears must be better than normal people's. "Did the thunder wake you, too?"

"I wasn't asleep."

Matt followed them up the stairs and down the hall to Jesse's room, hoping to tuck Jesse in and kiss him good-night again. He couldn't get enough of the normal stuff that most parents no doubt took for granted.

Another crack of thunder shook the house and Jesse wailed and reached for his mother. "I want to sleep with you."

"Okay, come on, sweetie."

Matt trailed along behind them to Jenny's room, curious. What was her room like? How was it decorated? With cowboy decals and wagon wheels? The thought gave him a chuckle.

When he walked into her bedroom, though, his mouth dropped open. He would never have taken Jenny for a lacy kind of girl, but there it was, on the bedspread and pillows scattered around the room and on the curtains. White lace everywhere.

Jenny set Jesse on the bed.

"I'm thirsty," he said while she wiped his tear-stained cheeks.

She turned to Matt. "Would you mind getting some water from the bathroom? The blue plastic cup is his."

Matt ran the water to get it cold, filled the cup and returned to the bedroom.

Jesse drank it down and Jenny placed it on the bedside table. She'd turned on a night-light plugged into an outlet near the door.

"Matt," Jesse said, "I need a good-night kiss."

Gladly.

Matt leaned over and kissed him, his small lips cool from the water, his breath smelling faintly of the popcorn they'd shared earlier in the bunkhouse.

Matt told him so.

"Don't tell Mom you putted butter on it," he whispered loudly enough for Jenny to hear every word. "She says it's just solid fat and clogs your arthuries."

Matt straightened and looked at her. Her hair was dark, shiny and bed mussed.

"Mommy, come into bed and Matt can kiss you goodnight, too."

Jenny blushed. "No, I'll get in after Matt leaves."

Jesse patted the bed beside him. "Come on, it's okay. Matt's really nice. You'll like it."

Lord, so will I, Matt thought.

He watched her cheeks flame and wondered what she would do.

She brushed past him and climbed under the covers. Seemed she'd do just about anything for her son.

Matt put his hands on either side of her head and leaned toward her. She watched him cautiously, the hazel highlights of her irises glinting in the yellow lamplight.

Eyes wide open, he brushed his lips over hers.

Her lips were soft and moist, her skin scented with lilacs. He recognized that scent. He'd smelled it on her before.

It was the closest he'd been to her in five years and he suddenly realized how much he'd missed his friend.

She'd known him better than anyone else on this earth, starting from those times they'd met under the

cotoneasters as kids, to talk about everything and anything, big and small.

He pulled away slowly.

"See, Mom?" his son said. "It's nice."

Yeah, so goddamn nice.

Matt stepped to the door and turned off the light,
Jenny's eyes tracking his every move.

He left the two most important people in his life
wrapped up cozily in her room and walked out of the
house into the cold downpour. He'd forgotten the raincoat. Didn't dare go back in. If he did, he wouldn't
leave a second time. He'd march back up the stairs and
into that bedroom, sit on that flowered armchair in the
corner and watch them sleep by the night-light until
dawn.

As he entered the bunkhouse, headlights swung
into the yard. Angus. Matt glanced at his watch. Three
o'clock.

Where the hell had Angus been all night?

CHAPTER EIGHT

ON FRIDAY, Hank and Amy and their two kids came over. Jenny had already mentioned that Matt could take an hour off to visit with them.

Matt shook Hank's hand and kissed Amy's cheek. Man, it felt good to see them again. He was introduced to their children.

Matt watched Amy and Jenny bustle off upstairs with Jenny's wedding dress. He'd forgotten about the wedding.

One more week. Could he stay and watch Jenny and Angus get married and then live on the same ranch with them?

He had no choice. It would be months before he'd worked off all that he owed Angus for those taxes.

Jesse ran up to greet Michael, then they took off together. To Matt, they looked the same age.

Amy's daughter, Cheryl, trailed after her mother and Jenny. She looked to be younger than her brother, Michael. Like her mother, she was going to be a real beauty when she grew up.

Matt and Hank leaned on the veranda's posts and faced the Circle K yard.

"You ever have trouble saying no to that little girl?" Matt asked.

Hank grinned. "All the time. I have to be real careful with her."

Matt turned confused eyes on Hank. "I'm a father, Hank, and I don't know what the hell I'm doing."

"So she told you," Hank said.

Matt nodded.

"We never asked her about it," Hank went on, "but Amy and I always knew it had to be you. She'd started that dumb argument with Amy about you, had run off and you'd chased her. The next morning you left the ranch. Didn't take Einstein to figure out you were the father. Why'd you run, Matt?"

Matt let out a breath. "I'm no good at getting serious with women."

Hank squeezed Matt's shoulder. "I'm glad you're back now."

Matt stared after his son. "It's a big responsibility. Does it ever scare you?"

"Not usually. My kid-raising philosophy is pretty simple."

"Yeah? What is it?"

"Love them like there's no tomorrow," Hank said in his familiar rusty growl.

Matt listened intently, wanting to learn secrets from a man he'd always admired and respected.

"Let them know they are loved," Hank continued, "every minute of every day."

Hank stopped there.

"That's it?" Matt asked. There had to more to it than that.

"Uh-huh," Hank replied. "Any mistakes you make will even out in the end."

Matt nodded. He'd felt loved for the first few years of

his life, before everything had changed with his mother. What if the rest of it hadn't happened? What if Matt had felt loved every day and the only mistakes his parents had made were normal ones. Too strict. Too lax. Love would make up for a lot of mistakes.

He shoved his hands into his pockets. If only he could get rid of this damn yearning.

Hank's son, Michael, ran onto the veranda with Jesse. The boys were almost the same age, but Michael was tall, like his father. Amy must've gotten pregnant pretty soon after she married Hank. Their love for each other looked good, real good.

Matt was glad things had worked out the way they had. For a while, before Amy and Hank had realized how much they loved each other, Matt had been interested in Amy. It would have been a fling, nothing more. He couldn't do more.

Then he'd spent that night with Jenny and realized where his heart belonged and what kind of trouble that would cause. And he'd run.

"Dad, Jesse and me are going to play outside," Michael said. "'Kay?"

"Yeah, have fun." Hank mussed his son's hair.

Jesse stood beside Matt, looking up at him, expectant.

Finally, he said, "We're going outside, okay?"

"Sure," Matt said.

Still, the boy waited for something. Matt reached out his hand, tentative and wondering whether this was what Jesse wanted, and mussed his hair. A great big grin split Jesse's face, then he took off after Michael.

Matt's heart flipped over. Affection and tenderness

oozed through his body along with wonderment. What had he done to deserve this boy?

Matt got beers for himself and Hank and sat on the veranda, watching their sons run in the yard.

Matt told Hank about the calf incident.

"There's been some cattle rustling over in the next county," Hank said. "Everyone's on alert. Let Angus know."

"Sure. There's no shortage of dishonest people in the world, is there?"

"No." Hank took a swig of his beer then said, "I'm putting my hands out riding the perimeter of the ranch all weekend."

"Even on a Sunday?"

"Yep, prime time for them to hit. Sheriff Kavenagh wants everyone vigilant for the next few weeks."

"Damn rustlers," Matt said, but without force. The day was too sunny and the beer too cold to worry about much.

"Angus might want to do the same," Hank said. "He's got the wealthiest ranch around."

"So the ranch hands won't get any days off this week."

"Nope."

Hollering from out behind the barn made them run. Jesse and Michael were screaming like they were being killed.

When Matt rounded the back corner of the barn, he stopped and stared.

Both boys lay on their backs in the manure corral, yelling their lungs out and crying.

Matt hustled to the fence. "Jesse, stand up real slow."

Jesse thrashed in the manure, setting up an aroma that threatened to gag Matt.

"Careful!" he said. "Don't get any more of that stuff on you than you already have."

Both boys stood, slowly, trying not to put their hands down in the decomposing manure, hands that were already covered to the wrists.

Their feet made sucking noises with each step they took toward the fence. Not that they had far to walk.

"What the heck were you two thinking?" Hank growled.

"We were just walking on the fence," Michael said.

"Yeah," Jesse piped up. "Like on a tightrope."

Probably one of them had dared the other to do it and they'd both ended up walking the top railing. One had lost his balance and then thrown off the other's balance. They'd landed in a pile of shit.

Matt remembered being that stupid when he was young. As if whatever *could* happen never would. Not to him, anyway.

He watched Jesse climb over the fence, just like Hank was making Michael do.

They marched the boys to the hose at the side of the house. Hank walked inside and shouted up the stairs, "Amy, Cheryl, it's time to go." He didn't sound the least bit happy. He rejoined Matt outside.

Matt turned the garden hose on low and sprayed Jesse.

"Ow!" Jesse cried. "That's cold."

Matt hardened his heart to his son's cries. "You fall into a manure pile," he said, raising his voice to be heard above the spraying water and his son's caterwauling, "you gotta expect to suffer for it."

"Why can't I just have a bath?" he wailed.

"Because you aren't walking into the house with shit all over you."

"I'm telling Mom on you," Jesse screamed. "You said 'shit.'"

"Yeah, well, at least I'm not wearing it."

"I don't like you," Jesse yelled.

It should have hurt, but somehow it didn't. Matt hid a smile and said, "Calm down."

"Your turn, Michael." Hank took the hose from Matt and turned it on his son, who started to yell.

"It's freezing! It's freezing!"

"What on earth happened?" Amy stood behind them, her hands on her hips. Jenny stood beside her with wide eyes.

"Your son fell in the manure pile," Hank said.

"*My* son?" Amy asked with a dangerous edge to her tone.

Hank turned to her, making sure his son didn't see the grin hovering around the corners of his mouth. "Your son," he repeated.

Amy suddenly looked as if she was trying not to smile, too.

They read each other well. For some reason, that fact intensified Matt's longing.

He turned to Jesse shivering and sobbing in the shade of the house, and said kindly, "Go stand in the sun and peel those clothes off."

"Not out here," he said, sounding more miserable than defiant. Matt caught the shy looks his son was casting toward Cheryl. Matt guessed her to be only a year younger than Jesse.

Did it really start that early? Shyness in front of a girl? He didn't remember.

"All right," he said. "Run around back and take them off. Then get inside for a bath."

Jesse took off.

"Leave those clothes on the grass," Matt called after him. "They're garbage."

Hank ordered Michael into the car. "No sitting. Stand up in the backseat. Don't put your bum anywhere near the upholstery."

Michael dragged his feet over to the car. "What can I hang on to?"

"My headrest."

Cheryl wrinkled her nose. "Do I gotta sit in the backseat with Michael?"

"Have to, honey. Do I have to?" Amy turned to Hank with a helpless little shrug.

"Put Cheryl on your lap," he said quietly. "We'll drive home real slow on the back roads."

Hank waved to Matt and Jenny. "See you two later."

He opened all the car's windows. Michael stood behind his father's seat and gripped the headrest, his face a picture of misery and humiliation. Cheryl and Amy climbed into the front seat. Hank started the car and pulled away at a crawl.

"Guess we'll be cleaning out that manure tomorrow. It's overdue," Jenny mumbled. "I'm going to run Jesse's bath."

Matt nodded, but didn't answer. He should go in to help her, but he didn't. He couldn't handle so domestic an incident with Jesse and Jenny. His emotions were all over the place these days, bad enough already without spending more time with them as if they were a real family.

One big thing relieved him—that he and Jesse were getting along so well. That this fatherhood business wasn't as tough as it looked.

He loved the daylights out of his son, and one day his son would love him in return.

Fatherhood was a breeze and pure, pure pleasure.

IT HAD STORMED badly Saturday night. On Sunday morning, deep puddles riddled the yard. Looked like they wouldn't be cleaning that manure lot today.

Matt watched Jesse and Jenny cross the yard toward the stable.

"Don't forget what I told you," Matt heard her say in a no-nonsense, I'm-telling-you-for-your-own-good kind of way. "No going anywhere near that creek. Do you hear me?"

"Mom, I want to get another frog. You said I could go today. Bucket's lonely."

The corner of Matt's mouth twitched. The frog's name still amused him.

"You can," Jenny said. "Just not today. The water will be running high and fast."

Jesse sighed and Matt chuckled to himself. The kid acted as if it was the end of the world.

When Jenny passed Matt, she said, "Can you help muck out the stalls? The other hands are repairing fences."

Matt followed her and picked up a rake to start working.

Jenny handed a kid's rake to Jesse.

"You do Flora's stall."

"Her name's Butter," Jesse grumbled.

While Jenny and Matt herded horses out into the corral, Jesse halfheartedly raked old straw.

They worked quietly for an hour.

"You want a glass of iced tea?" Jenny asked Matt.

"Yeah. I'd appreciate it," he answered, swiping his sleeve across his forehead. It was a warm morning.

"Jesse," Jenny called, "do you want something cold to drink?"

Matt heard her walk to Flora's stall.

"Jesse?" she called.

No answer, then, "Have you seen Jesse?"

Matt looked up. She was asking him, with a crease of concern wrinkling her forehead.

"No. I thought he was raking the stall."

Jenny ran out of the barn, calling her son's name.

Still no answer.

Matt had a bad feeling about this and walked outside.

Jenny rushed into the house, still calling for Jesse. A minute later she ran back out and to the horses in the corral.

"What's happening?" Matt called.

"He snuck away. He's probably at the creek. He wanted another frog so much." Fear permeated her voice. "I shouldn't have told him not to go. That just made him want to go more. It'll be bad down there."

Matt jumped the fence and ran to Masterpiece, hauling himself onto his horse by a fistful of mane.

He rode bareback out to Still Creek, which was anything but still. It roiled from the night's downpour and overflowed its banks in some places.

Matt's heart lodged in his throat, a great lump of

panic that made swallowing hard. A little kid like Jesse wouldn't stand a chance in the writhing current.

Matt raced along the bank. Nothing. What if the boy had come down here and been swept away? Would they be searching for a dead body?

Oh, God, no.

Matt chased the movement of the water downstream. He and Master flew over sodden ground. He stared at the banks, afraid of what he might see, what he might find.

A sound that might have been his name caught his attention and his gaze shot up toward the middle of the creek.

What he saw filled him with icy panic.

Jesse stood on a flat rock, surrounded by rushing water.

Alive! Thank God!

He hadn't drowned, but the stone couldn't have been wider than three feet. Matt's blood ran cold.

Tears streamed down Jesse's face, along with snot and what looked like a bit of vomit on his chin. He was cold and trembling.

He'd been vomiting up water. Lord. Lord.

Matt jumped from Master's back. "Jesse, don't move," he called. "Stay as still as you can."

Jesse didn't respond, just kept crying.

"Did you hear me?" Matt yelled. "Don't move. Nod if you can hear me."

Jesse nodded. His skin was pale and he was trembling, but he stood still as Matt had asked him to.

Jenny's voice carried on the wind as she rode up to the water's edge, her screams blood churning.

Jesse wailed harder and Matt motioned to Jenny to be quiet.

"Jesse," he said, his voice urgent, "don't move."

Matt ran to Jenny and Lacey. She'd saddled Lacey before riding out. She'd also thrown a blanket across her thighs and a rope on top of that.

Smart girl. Even in her fear, she'd been rational enough to bring the right things.

Matt grabbed the rope and tied it around the trunk of a Russian olive. A two-inch thorn pierced his shoulder. He tied the other end of the rope around his waist.

He waded into the stream, buffeted by the insistent current that urged, *Go this way. Follow me.*

Managing to stay his course, Matt stopped five feet away from the rock. The rope was too short.

He let loose a string of curses. Making sure his footing was sound, he untied the rope from his waist.

Holding the last six inches of it, he spread his arms. He still couldn't reach. Damn!

He could tell Jesse to jump, but what if he couldn't jump that far? What if Matt missed?

By some miracle, Jesse had survived falling into this maelstrom once. They wouldn't be so lucky a second time.

Matt let go of the rope altogether.

The current was wicked and strong, but Matt made it to the rock.

He lifted Jesse against his chest and told him to hang on tight.

When he felt sure of his footing again, he set out for the bank of the stream. Water buffeted him and, like a willful child, tried to make him do what it wanted him to. To change course. To rush downstream. To go with the crazy, frothing flow.

His foot slipped on a submerged rock and they went under. Matt's arms clenched around Jesse and he pushed them both to the surface. Jesse coughed up water and more vomit.

Matt gagged on the water he'd swallowed. Jesse's arms were wrapped around his throat tightly enough to choke him.

The stream carried them too far before Matt could grab a handful of weeping-willow branches. One arm still clutched Jesse and the other clung to the tree for all he was worth.

He heard Jenny ride up on Lacey, but Lacey refused to ride into the Russian olives on the other side of the willow. The horse knew that the thorns would tear her hide to pieces.

"I'm tying the rope to Lacey's saddle," Jenny called.

A minute later, she was forcing her way through the thorns of the olive trees with loops of rope curled around one hand.

"Jesse," Matt ordered, "I need you to keep your arms and legs wrapped around me. I have to let go of you for a minute."

"No!" Jesse cried.

"I need you to be a big boy for me now. Okay?"

Jesse nodded, but uncertainly.

"I'll keep you safe," Matt whispered against his ear. "Nothing is going to happen to you while I'm here with you. Understand?"

"Yeah," Jesse whispered back. He was shuddering

in Matt's arms from equal parts terror and cold. The water was freezing.

Jesse's teeth chattered.

"When I count to three," Matt told him, "I want you to squeeze me real tight."

He told Jenny what he was doing.

"One...two...three...now!"

She tossed the rope to Matt. Jesse choked him and he held his breath so he wouldn't gag. He snagged the end of the rope.

"Got it," he yelled.

Working quickly, he knotted the rope tightly around his waist. Hand over hand, he pulled on the rope and got himself and Jesse out of the water and onto the muddy bank.

It felt unstable, so he continued to pull until he reached Jenny.

Jesse wailed and reached for his mother. Jenny took him in her arms.

Her son clung to her like a leech.

Jenny turned to go back through the olive trees, but they got caught in her hair. Jesse cried out. One of the thorns must have stuck him.

"Wait," Matt said.

Jenny came back to him.

He peeled off his jacket and then his shirt, and handed the denim shirt to Jenny. "Put this around you. The second layer will protect you."

He told Jesse to hang on to him again, just like he had in the river. Jesse wrapped himself around Matt's bare torso. Matt slipped his arms through the jacket backward so Jesse would be protected.

Pushing the collar up to cover Jesse's head, he dived through the trees, wincing as thorns scored his back.

The jacket and his arms protected Jesse.

Jenny waited on the other side with the blanket and bundled Jesse into it after Matt took off the jacket.

While Jesse cried, Jenny held her son in her arms, squeezing her eyes closed. She whispered his name.

Matt bent over with his hands on his knees, trying to stop shaking, feeling about as substantial as a dried-out leaf tossed about by the wind.

Somehow, Jesse must have been swept up onto the rock. If he hadn't, Matt would have been searching for his body. Or, if he'd hit his head on the rock instead of being tossed onto it, he would have drowned. Still, Matt would have been looking for a tiny dead body.

Jenny said, "Hold Jesse," and handed the child to him while she mounted her horse.

Now that Jesse was safe in his arms and the danger was past, a fear larger and deeper than Matt had ever known swept through him. With it came pure cleansing anger that washed the sharp edges of his shock and panic away.

"Don't you ever, ever go near the stream again without an adult," Matt said from behind tightly clamped teeth. He gave Jesse a shake, not rough, but not gentle either.

"Do you understand?" he asked.

Jesse howled.

This was awful, *awful,* this pain of parenthood, this danger of losing a child. Why did people have children willingly? Why did they *choose* to put themselves through this? Were all parents insane?

Jenny leaned down and took Jesse away from Matt.

Jesse whimpered and pointed at Matt. "I don't like you."

"Shh," Jenny said, her voice shaky. "Matt just saved your life."

She made sure he was snug and safe on her lap, and completely covered by the blanket.

She glanced at Matt and mouthed, *Thank you.* No sound came out, but he read her lips.

"Let's get back to the house," he said, shrugging into his wet jacket.

He whistled for Master, who grazed in a meadow. The horse trotted over and Matt rode home.

He'd lost his temper, badly. Had Jesse deserved what Matt had given him? Or was Matt becoming like his mother—unreasonable and crazy?

The anger he'd felt had come from purely primal fear. Terror. Jesse was lucky to be alive. Had Matt gone overboard? He didn't know.

At the house, Jenny carried Jesse inside while Matt took care of the horses. He finished mucking out the last of the stalls, giving himself time to calm down before he went in to see how Jesse was doing. When he was ready, he changed into dry clothes and headed toward the house.

JENNY SAT on the sofa with a clean, dry child on her lap who was dead to the world. Matt winced. Terrible thing to think at this time.

She feathered her fingers through her son's hair as if she couldn't stop touching him. Matt was sure there must have been a time when his mother had done that to him, when he must have felt as safe and protected as Jesse was now.

He couldn't remember.

Jesse had a couple of bandages on his hands where thorns had gotten him.

Matt sat down next to Jenny, touched one of the bandages and whispered, "Are these the only scratches he got?"

"Yes, thank goodness."

"How is he?"

"Scared. Exhausted. I only managed to get a little soup and hot chocolate into him before he fell asleep. He'll probably be out for a couple of hours."

Matt leaned against the back of the sofa then hissed in a breath and shot forward.

"What's wrong?" Jenny's face showed alarm.

"Olive thorns tore me apart."

"Let me see." She shifted to put Jesse on the sofa, but Matt stopped her with a hand on her arm.

"Don't disturb him."

"I really need to look at your back." She pointed to the spots of blood he'd left on the beige upholstery. His blood had soaked through his clean shirt.

"Come," Jenny ordered.

Matt followed her upstairs to the bathroom. She put down the toilet lid and told him to sit with his back to the sink.

Jenny gasped when she saw his damaged skin. "Why didn't you say something earlier? You're a mess."

She rummaged in the cupboards and found a bunch of bandages. "I'm so sorry this happened."

With a clean washcloth and warm water, she cleansed his wounds.

"You're covered with deep scratches," she said.

Matt flinched when she touched them. "They sting like a bugger."

"Sorry to make them feel worse, but we need them to be clean so you don't get an infection."

She dabbed the scratches with antibiotic cream. Matt tried not to notice how good her hands felt on him, but it was hard.

He tried not to notice, too, how her hands slowed, as though maybe she liked it as much as he did.

Gently, she covered his back with gauze pads, securing them with tape.

Jenny had always been a wild child, impulsive, sometimes defensive, and often crazy, but he remembered how she had also always been tender and gentle with the children they took care of at the Sheltering Arms.

He appreciated that tenderness now, but knew it was nothing more than gratitude on her part. Since he'd come home, she'd been nothing but distant with him.

He had saved their child today, though. He just wished he hadn't been so hard on Jesse. The boy was only four.

"Listen," Matt said when she'd finished. "I'm really sorry I yelled at Jesse. That I got so mad."

"He deserved it. If you hadn't yelled at him, I would have. It's a natural reaction to the fear."

Jenny packed away the first-aid kit. "Today was completely my fault. I should have watched him more closely."

"Hey, remember how some of the kids on the Sheltering Arms could be so unpredictable?"

"Yes, but not one of them ever came this close to drowning."

Her eyes were huge and still held traces of the fear he'd seen in her down by the stream.

He brushed her arm and she hissed and jerked away.

"I'm not going to jump your bones," he said, angry now. "Haven't I shown you that you can trust me?"

Jenny held up a staying hand. "It's just a scratch I haven't tended yet."

Matt's anger changed direction. "Why not? Why did you do mine first? Are there more? Let me see how bad they are."

Jenny shied away. "I can take care of them."

"Did you get any on your back?"

She shrugged. "I might have."

"Let me see." His tone brooked no argument from her. "Now."

She unbuttoned her blouse, turned away from him and slipped it partway down her back. The thorns had gotten her, all right. Four long scratches marred her shoulders.

He picked up a clean facecloth and soaked it in hot water. She stood still while he cleansed her wounds, but he knew they hurt. She'd always been stoic and stronger than anyone he knew.

Jenny held her shirt up over her breasts, so he couldn't tell how bad she was at the front.

Matt got the kit back out of the cupboard and applied the antibiotic cream to the scratches. Her skin and his fingers warmed it quickly. He'd forgotten about her skin, about how soft it was.

He ran his finger down her spine and she shivered.

Maybe she was remembering, too, how good they'd

been together that night. But that was then and this was now.

Nothing would happen here between them.

He reined himself in and stepped away from her.

"Can you get the rest yourself?" he asked.

"No problem." Her voice didn't sound as nonchalant as her words did.

"What's going on?" The deep voice from the hallway startled them both. Angus.

Great, Matt thought, this looks bad. Both he and Jenny had their shirts off.

Matt turned his back to Angus and pointed over his shoulder to his bandages. "Russian olive thorns."

Jenny pulled her shirt all the way on and buttoned it. Then she rolled up her sleeves to bare her arms, where the thorns had left livid scratches.

"What on earth were the two of you doing in those trees?"

Jenny bit her lip.

"Jesse nearly drowned today."

Then the woman who'd been so calm and strong throughout the ordeal turned toward the sink and vomited.

CHAPTER NINE

SOMETHING HAD CHANGED between Matt and Jenny since this morning. She'd dropped the hostility, the distance. Maybe because they'd lived through a harrowing experience? Matt didn't know for sure why, but he felt his barriers fall with hers.

"How do people survive having kids?" he asked her after dinner in the stable as they groomed the horses properly. Matt had done only a rough job earlier. "Why do they put themselves through so much?"

Jenny ran her long fingers down Masterpiece's nose. "What do you think of Master?"

Huh? "What do I think of my horse?"

"Yes. Do you care about him? Or is he just a tool you need to get your work done on the ranch? Do you also have affection for him?"

"Me and Master are a team. You know that, Jenny. I love that horse."

"You do know that he won't live forever? That someday you will have to say goodbye to him?"

"What's your point?"

"When Master dies, will you refuse to buy another horse because it hurts too much to lose him?"

"Of course not. I'll need another one and I'll start to like him as much as I like Master."

"Right. Despite being a workhorse, he also enriches

your life just by his existence and by how much pleasure you derive from each other's company and from your rides across the prairie."

"Okay."

"What if Jesse came to you and asked you for a dog?" Jenny asked. "Would you tell him he couldn't have one because someday the dog would die?"

"Of course not."

Jenny scratched Master's neck and the horse closed his eyes. "Jesse enriches my life."

Matt stood and watched Jenny charm his horse.

"It would be horribly painful to lose him," she continued. "If he died, for a long time afterward, I would probably believe that life was no longer worth living, but I would never regret having had him just because his loss had caused me so much grief and anger."

"But how do you deal with the fear?" Matt asked. "You know that at any moment, on any given day, something bad could happen to Jesse."

"Yes." Jenny shivered. "Most days I don't think about it. I just live my life with him as if the bad things won't happen. After his near drowning, though, it'll be hard to relax for a few days."

Jenny smiled sadly. She still looked pale but seemed to have gotten some of her strength back. She left the stable and went into the house.

She'd apologized many times this morning for vomiting, as if she wasn't allowed to be human, as though she had to be strong at all times. Why was she so hard on herself?

Matt got what she had meant about loving and losing, totally understood, but just didn't think he could live constantly on edge, constantly fearing he would lose his child.

He wasn't strong enough to be a parent.

And yet, he was one.

Jesse ran down the aisle, trailing a long rope behind him. He seemed to have recovered his equilibrium pretty darn quickly.

"Can you show me some roping and riding now?" Jesse said, as happy and eager as if today's near disaster had never happened. "I can ride a horse."

"You can ride a pony," Matt said. Maybe kids were really resilient, but he wasn't.

"Can I learn how to rodeo on Butter?"

"No, you don't start to learn on horseback."

"How do I start?"

Matt didn't want this intimacy, not anymore. Not after the shit-kicking his nerves had taken.

He should tell Jenny to teach her son how to rodeo. He should walk away now with his sanity intact. He should leave, just as Jenny had predicted he would.

Jesse watched him with hero worship in his eyes.

Aw, kid, I'm no hero.

Matt couldn't help himself. He took the rope from Jesse then frowned. "This one's awfully big for you. We need to get you a kid's rope."

"I'm gonna ask for one for Christmas."

"Christmas? That's too far away. You need a little plastic calf's head to stick in the hay. Your mom gonna get you one of those, too?"

Jesse shrugged.

"Let's ride over to Hank's ranch," Matt said. "He's got all that stuff. We can borrow some from him."

They wandered across the yard together and entered the house.

"Jenny?" Matt called.

Angela stepped out of the kitchen, wiping her hands on a dish towel. "She just left to get me something from town.

"Look at you two. Like two peas in a pod." She smiled.

Peas in a pod? Matt looked down at the blond-haired boy beside him. Not quite. While Matt still reeled with this morning's terror, Jesse was ready for the next adventure. "I need to slip over to the Sheltering Arms to talk to Hank about something. I'm taking Jesse with me. Okay?"

"Sure," Angela said. "He'll like that. Right, Jesse?"

"Uh-huh."

"Okay, off with you. I'll tell Jenny where he is."

Matt left the house with Jesse in tow.

They returned an hour later with a small rope of Jesse's own. Jesse clutched it in one fist. He had his other arm wrapped around a plastic calf's head.

They stuck the calf's head in a bale of hay and took it onto the lawn.

Jesse roped for two hours straight. The tip of his tongue stuck out of the side of his mouth and drool ran down his chin. By the end of the afternoon, he was hitting the target more often than he missed. The kid had real staying power.

Matt didn't. He was terrified that he didn't have what it took to nurture a kid and stick around. The outcome could be so damn painful. If Jesse died, Matt knew he wouldn't be able to survive the grief. Yes, he knew most kids grew up just fine, but Jesse had clearly inherited Jenny's stubborn wild streak. He would take risks and Matt knew he wouldn't be able to cope with the consequences.

Best thing to do was to keep his distance.

He felt himself grow cold and withdraw from his son. It broke his heart after all they'd shared.

Jesse was watching him with his head cocked to one side. "Whatsa matter?"

Matt couldn't answer.

Jenny pulled into the yard and waved.

Jesse waved back.

Matt turned and walked away.

Jesse could explain to his mother what they'd been doing. Jenny could take over his rodeo training now.

Matt went to the bunkhouse and threw himself onto his cot.

A few minutes later, Jenny came in. "Thanks for teaching Jesse how to rope."

"No problem." He sounded short. Tense.

"What's going on?"

"I can't— After this morning, I can't be the father Jesse needs." He sat up. "You were right about me. I don't have the guts for the job."

"Until now, you've been doing really well." That admission looked as if it cost Jenny a lot. "You can still get to know him more."

"That's quite a statement coming from you." Matt smiled grimly. "You should be pleased. You've never wanted me here, or anywhere near my son. Now I'm agreeing with you that I'm not good for him and you want me to get to know him even more."

"True."

"Listen, compared to me, you are Mother Teresa. You're the best damn parent a boy could want. I can't measure up to that."

A look crossed Jenny's face that Matt could only interpret as...self-recrimination.

"What?" he asked.

Jenny sat on the cot across from his. "I'm not so great. I have to tell you something. It's been eating away at me."

"What?"

She stared at her hands, took her time weaving her fingers together. "I did something terrible and I've been ashamed of myself ever since."

"Jenny, spit it out. How bad can it be?"

"Pretty bad. That night in your parents' cabin?"

Matt nodded.

"I planned the whole thing. I pretended to be angry with you for being attracted to Amy. I set up that argument with her so you would be the one to come after me."

"Because you wanted to sleep with me? I figured that out already."

"No, because I wanted to get pregnant and I wanted you to be the father."

Matt sucked in a breath. She had to be kidding.

"Why?" he shouted and the air whooshed out of him, leaving him stunned and empty. "We talked for *hours* about how rotten my parents were. I told you I didn't want kids."

"Yes," Jenny whispered. "But I loved you with all my heart, and I knew I would feel the same way about your children."

"So you always planned to be a single parent?"

Her cheeks reddened. "No, I thought that once I was pregnant, you'd marry me."

"So you wanted to trap me into marriage?" She reached a hand toward him, but he recoiled. "You knew how I felt about marriage."

"I know." She lifted her chin and her tone became defiant. "You were my best friend. I didn't understand how you could believe that anything we had would be wrong."

She jumped up from the cot. "I was tired of waiting for you."

Matt cradled his head in his hands. "And now I have a son without ever deciding I wanted one." His voice came out muffled. "You made that decision for both of us."

"You didn't *have* to sleep with me."

"After I saw you naked in the cabin I wasn't thinking too clearly."

"I was. I plotted the whole thing. I was regular like clockwork and I knew there was a good chance I'd get pregnant." She looked and sounded regretful. "The choice I made for both of us was wrong."

Jenny's words sounded thick and Matt looked up. Her chin trembled.

Oh, Lord, don't cry. I'm not in a forgiving mood.

"I don't regret Jesse," she went on, setting her jaw so it wouldn't shake. "I do regret not being honest with you. You deserved better from me."

She left the bunkhouse before he could respond.

Matt couldn't take it in. Jenny was the most ethical person he knew, but she'd lied to him. Not in a little white-lie kind of way, but in a huge, screwing-with-someone-else's-life kind of way.

He couldn't get his head around it so gave up trying, but for the rest of the day, Matt kept his distance from her.

From Jesse, too.

LATE SUNDAY AFTERNOON, an ominous light hovered over the silent landscape. Not a creature stirred. No birds chirped. A couple of raindrops fell. Looked like it was going to be a bad storm.

Matt rode along the boundary between the Circle K and the Sheltering Arms. Last night, Angus and Jenny had decided to err on the side of safety and get everyone out patrolling the ranch.

A half hour ago, Matt had called Angus on his cell because he hadn't liked what he saw brewing on the horizon.

Angus wanted to patrol until six o'clock. He was certain the storm would hold off until then.

Staring around him, Matt knew Angus was wrong. The storm was almost on top of them and they should all head back. The prairie was no place to be caught in a thunderstorm.

His radio crackled and Hip's voice came over, yelling, "We've got cattle being stolen."

Matt swore.

Angus responded on the radio. "Where?"

"Just past the old quarry," Hip said. "They don't know Will and me are watching them. We can take them by surprise."

"Wait for us," Jenny said. "They could be dangerous."

"Let's catch these bastards." Angus's voice was strong despite the static.

They converged from different directions until they rode abreast, Will and Hip on ATVs and the rest on horseback, their horses' hooves driving a demanding beat.

When they came up over the rise Hip directed them to, they saw five men on horseback below herding about twenty head of Circle K cattle away from Angus's property.

"Hell," Jenny yelled.

"Shit," Matt swore.

"Let's get them," Angus shouted, then spurred his horse.

They took off, but the second the rustlers heard them coming, they abandoned the cattle and rode away, hard and fast, three of them veering off to the left, two of them to the right. Splitting up.

Damn.

"Hip! Will! We'll take the three on the left," Angus yelled, his words blown behind him by a cold wind swirling across the prairie.

He pointed to Matt and Jenny. "You take those two."

Matt cursed, but couldn't think about how he didn't want to be anywhere near this woman. He needed to focus on the chase. They were delayed by having to ride around the herd then pick up the trail farther on. Bastards. He couldn't let them get away. He leaned forward, almost level with Master's neck.

The sky darkened, and the afternoon descended into a gray-green twilight. Fat drops of rain hit Matt square in the face. He brushed them away and rode like a demon. There was no way he was losing those guys. Angus depended on him to catch them.

"Matt," he heard Jenny call through the roar of the wind that had grown steadily worse.

"What?" he called back, not breaking speed.

"Look!" she shouted.

He turned back to her then looked where she pointed. Damn. The howling wind had saplings bent nearly to the ground and was stripping mature trees of leaves and smaller branches. A solid wall of rain was coming right at them. Within seconds, he was drenched to the skin. Jenny looked no better, but she could drown for all he cared, his anger at her sharp and righteous. He slowed Master, then pulled up. Too hard to see the ground in front of him.

The chase was over before it had even begun. They wouldn't catch anyone today. Frustration ate at Matt, but there was no sane choice but to stop. They'd ridden too far to return to the Kinsey house in this rain. They couldn't even head to his old house on the far side of the ranch.

"Where can we go?" he asked, but his words were blown away by the wind.

Jenny and Lacey sidled closer. "What?" she yelled. She looked as frustrated as he felt.

"Where-can-we-go?" He enunciated and she read his lips.

"Back to the ranch."

"Are you crazy? We could get hit by lightning out here."

He saw the uncertainty in her eyes and knew it wasn't about lightning. She didn't want to be alone with him, either.

A shaft of lightning hit the earth a hundred yards in front of them and sent up the scent of scorched earth.

The hair rose on Matt's arms. Master reared on his hind legs to turn away, but Matt held him steady with his thighs.

Lacey skittered away. Jenny forced her back beside Master.

Matt yelled, "What's around here?" He knew Jenny had traveled every inch of this terrain over the years.

She looked around wildly. He knew she was trying to come up with some alternative to being trapped with him.

Her hat flew off and hit him in the chest. He caught it—just—then shoved it inside his shirt. He snuggled his own hat down hard on his head. The wind whipped rain under his brim, stinging his skin. He turned away from it.

He looked at Jenny. "Where?" he shouted. "Hurry."

Jenny said something he couldn't catch, then pointed. She might have said "MacCaffery," but he wasn't sure. When he tried to ask, he got a mouthful of rain. Then he remembered the small cabin the MacCafferys had on the back end of their property, put there for ranch hands who spent nights on the range.

He spurred Master and followed Jenny. She rode hard and fast into the sheeting rain. By the time they finally found the cabin, his breath came out of him in gusts.

Jenny pulled up around the far side of a ramshackle cabin he could barely make out in the downpour and quickly dismounted. She and Matt secured the horses on the leeward side of the small building under a small lean-to, out of the worst of the wind. Thunder cracked overhead, close by. They whipped the saddles off the horses, rubbed the animals down as best they could with their sleeves, then ran for the entrance.

Warped by the elements, the door stuck. Matt put his shoulder against it and shoved it open with a high screech. Jenny shut the door behind them and latched it. They stood in the dark, panting in the stale, musty air.

Damn. This couldn't be happening. Déjà vu all over again and he hated it. He'd rather be anywhere than trapped in a cabin with Jenny Sterling. Judging by the building's small exterior, it was only a one-room cabin.

Matt let his eyes adjust to what little light filtered in through the windows. Lightning flashed, illuminating the room for a split second. In that brief moment, he saw enough to know they were in a rudimentary cabin little better than a shack. It had a fireplace, though, a necessity for stranded ranch hands.

If the storm blew through quickly enough, they could ride home. At any rate, that's what Matt prayed would happen.

Matt tried to raise Angus on the radio, but it was dead. He pulled out his cell phone and managed to get through to tell him where they were.

He shuffled toward the fireplace. He heard Jenny creep along the far wall and rummage around on a table or counter. He heard pots moving. Then she struck a match and lit an oil lantern, illuminating that end of the shack.

"Toss those matches over here," Matt said. He caught them easily when she did. She'd always had a good arm. He knelt beside the fireplace. His soaked jeans stuck to his skin, pulling at the hairs on his legs.

"Cold in here," he said, trying to make normal conversation.

"No fooling," Jenny answered and he heard her teeth chatter.

Matt sorted through a stack of wood, found shreds for kindling and a couple of smaller logs. He set them up in the fireplace then put a match to them.

When he stood, he noticed a pack of cigarettes on the rough-hewn mantel and picked them up. He blew off a layer of dust and sneezed. Must've been here at least a year, he guessed.

He threw the empty pack into the burgeoning fire, where it flared and crinkled, then burned to ash.

The storm raged around the cabin, thunder shaking its walls and wind whistling through its cracks, but inside, the intimacy was broken only by the crackle of the fire and the sound of Jenny rummaging in the cupboards.

"Find anything?" he asked.

She held up a can of coffee and some tinned beans, her mouth set in a thin line and her eyes not quite natural. If he hadn't known Jenny for the fearless creature she was, he would have said she was terrified of being alone with him. Like this.

Her wet shirt clung to her, molded her breasts like a second skin, or a man's hands. Matt shuddered and turned back to the fire.

It was so damn stupid to get trapped like this.

He couldn't repeat what happened five years ago. In his worst nightmares, he hadn't imagined that he would ever be stuck alone with Jenny in a cabin again, in a storm, with no escape. Even his rage didn't feel like enough to keep him away from her. He gripped the edge of the mantel.

"MacCaffery's boys obviously use this place at times." Jenny sounded as strained as he felt. Matt stared at her. She pointed to the tins in the cupboard and the jar of instant coffee.

He said nothing.

A gust of wind rattled the windows and Jenny shivered.

"We need to dry our clothes," she said.

Not this again. Not this.

Jenny walked to the door and claimed a couple of oilskin coats hanging from a hook behind it.

"These are old but they'll have to do."

She dragged two rickety ladder-back chairs from a small table and set them next to the fire.

"You want to build that fire up real high?" she said.

He watched her over his shoulder and willed her to move, to take off her clothes.

Reading the heat in his eyes accurately, Jenny waited for him to look away. He turned away from her slowly, and added a log to the fire.

"Don't look," Jenny said.

Matt stared into the fire. *Don't turn around. For God's sake, don't look.*

He clenched his fists and rested one of them on the hearth, letting the stone dig into his knuckles so the pain in his hand would be stronger than in his heart. And in his loins.

He heard the soft rustle of fabric and knew that half of Jenny's clothes had just fallen to the floor. He kept staring blindly into the flickering flames as though his life depended on it. As angry as he was with Jenny, as much as he hated what she'd done in the past, he still wanted her—and chastised himself for that.

His body didn't know the difference between then and now, the old Jenny and the new, the past betrayal that colored the present. His body knew only what it wanted at this moment. Jenny.

"You can turn around now." She wore one of the coats and draped her clothes over the back of a chair, hanging a skimpy piece of pink lace over one of the arms and a pink lace bra over the other.

Matt clenched his jaw.

She stepped toward the hearth to stoke the fire. Her coat brushed his arm and he jerked away.

She flinched. "Your turn to change," she said, her tone ringing with equal parts defiance and hurt.

Matt untucked his shirt from his pants. Everything stuck to his skin and felt clammy. He peeled his pants down his legs then put on the coat. It was stiff. He wondered how Jenny could stand it against her own soft skin. He remembered that skin—how it felt like satin, but softer; like silk, but warmer.

"Are you hungry?" Jenny asked, her voice tentative. He hated that. He couldn't fight with a hesitant or hurt or vulnerable Jenny, and he really needed to fight with her. Or else he was going to take her in his arms and kiss the daylights out of her, drown himself in her. Why was love so frigging hard?

Love? Déjà vu was right.

JENNY STARED at Matt. This was her worst nightmare. Her absolute worst nightmare. What quirk of fate had them here alone? She didn't care how they got here. She just knew she couldn't let history repeat itself.

Five years ago, she had shaped their night together to come out one way. She could shape this night to turn out very differently.

She turned away from Matt to busy herself along the wall that could be called a kitchen only by a stretch of the imagination. She found a can opener some cowboy had left behind at one point—as old as the hills and hard to use—and jabbed the sharp end into the top of the tin of beans. It hurt her wrist and took all her strength to cut around the top of the can, but she'd be damned if she'd ask Matt for help.

At the fireplace, she dumped the beans into a pot and placed it on the hearth to warm slowly. She found a couple of plates, chipped around the rims, and set a fork onto each.

Finished with as many chores as she could think of to distract herself, Jenny stood and stared out the window at a dark, angry landscape. The thunder had moved on, but rain still hammered the tin roof of the cabin.

She felt Matt's eyes on her. *Stop. Don't look at me.* She'd already seen the heat of anger, and more. Lust. Passion.

When she turned back to him, she found him a foot away, staring at her. Just staring, his eyes full of anger and confusion. The confusion broke her. She'd hurt him badly. Worse than she would have ever thought.

"I'm sorry," she whispered. "I'm so sorry."

In spite of her righteousness and her fear, she could no longer deny that what she'd done was wrong. That she shouldn't have tried to trap him. That she should have told him the truth as soon as she knew she was pregnant.

It had been a knee-jerk response to the worry that Matt couldn't possibly be any better than his crazy parents. That he wouldn't stick around for her any more than he would have for Elsa. He'd already proved that by running away after that night. Or so she'd believed at the time.

"I'm sorry," she whispered again. She'd known Matt well as a child. On that hill lined with cotoneasters, they'd talked so often, about everything, including his twisted family, trying to make sense of a world that was often senseless.

Matt grabbed her, hauled her against his chest and kissed her with a fierce passion that matched the depth of her remorse. His fingers bit into her upper arms. She struggled against him, not to get away, but to get closer, to crawl into his skin if she could, to comfort him, and to seek his absolution for the terrible things she'd done.

The kiss was rough and hard, not at all the way he'd kissed her five years ago. His tongue probed the corners of her mouth. His arms became steel bands across her back. His erection pushed against her belly and she welcomed it.

She needed this. Wrapping her arms around his neck, she pressed herself against him, absorbing his scent, dizzy with passion. Matt. Oh, Matt.

He broke the kiss, leaving her lips wet and cold. He shoved the fingers of one hand into her hair and cupped the back of her head. His heart hammered against her chest, his breath warmed her temple.

He shook and she trembled with him. Then he was

dragging her onto the floor in front of the fire, lying on top of her, heavy and solid and so welcome. He clawed at the buttons on her coat. She clawed at his, touched his hot skin. He pulled her nipple into his mouth and her eyes flew open.

No!

What was she doing? She was going to marry Angus at the end of the week, and here she was on the floor with Matt again.

She had no sense where Matt was concerned.

He pulled her wrists above her head and she squirmed beneath him. No.

"Matt, no."

He didn't hear her, just sucked on her nipple harder, sending shards of response through her belly. She shuddered then held herself taut. She couldn't do this with Matt while Angus trusted her so deeply.

"Matt." She wriggled one arm free and grabbed his hair. "No!"

MATT OPENED HIS EYES, struggled to understand what Jenny was saying, winced at the pain at his temple. She had hold of a fistful of his hair and pulled it hard enough to keep his head away from her.

"What," he mumbled, trying to break out of the angry, horny daze he was in. "What?"

She repeated what she'd been yelling at him, but quietly now. "No."

"Why not?" he demanded, breathing his frustration into her face.

"Angus." She said the only word she knew would make sense to Matt at this moment.

He rolled off her and away, until he came up hard against the chairs. They screeched across the floor.

He let out a cry of pure, impotent frustration but kept away from her as he brought himself back under control.

Jenny rolled over to face the fire, trembling with her needs and overwhelming emotions. She needed Matt in one way, and Angus in another, but she couldn't have both, and she would never, ever betray Angus.

The stress that had built in her since Matt had returned boiled over and tears threatened, but she fought them. She wasn't a crying kind of girl.

She'd had only two sexual encounters with Matt. One had been better than she'd ever dreamed it would be. Tonight, it was so much less and she mourned her loss.

THE STORM STILL RAGED outside, but Matt's inner storm had calmed.

Staring at the ceiling, Matt realized the truth he'd been hiding from himself. He loved Jenny. He had since that night they'd spent together.

No. He'd loved her for years before that.

He was filled with such an aching, beautiful love for her that it pained him. It was so much more than the lust that had just overwhelmed him.

She'd lied to him, twice, yet still he loved her and always would. He admired her strength and her honesty. She could have never told him that she'd gotten pregnant on purpose and he would have been none the wiser. But as soon as he'd praised her, she'd had to be honest.

She wasn't his. He didn't want her to marry Angus, but he wouldn't marry her himself.

He'd been running scared for a long time. He wasn't afraid for himself, though.

He feared for Jenny. In this moment when he *knew* that if he tried hard enough he could seduce her, he became noble. For this one night, he became more than his father had ever taught him to be, and more than he'd thought he was.

He could do the right thing and leave Jenny to her dreams. She could live a better life without him to screw it up for her the way Long men had been doing for generations.

Matt might have thought that he had grown now that he'd met his son, that the experience might have matured him, but he knew better.

After his reaction to Jesse's near drowning, he realized he still didn't have the courage for long-term, lifetime relationships.

With a concerted effort to overcome his fear, he would stay in his son's life, but watch Jenny from afar.

She stirred beside him and he felt her shoulders shake.

"Are you crying?" Never, not once in his years of knowing her, not even after she'd lost her home, had Matt seen her cry.

"No," she said.

"I don't believe you."

She rolled toward him. "I'm not lying and I'm not crying. I'm trying *not* to cry."

He started to laugh. That was Jenny, defiant and resistant and resilient. He couldn't stand to leave her alone.

"Come here," he whispered, because as much as she'd

been wrong and as deeply as she'd hurt him, she needed him. And he needed her.

Jenny went straight into the arms he opened for her, and burrowed against his chest.

"I'm so sorry," she whispered. He heard the truth in the words.

"I know," he said and kissed her temple. "I know." He felt old and tired, but cleansed. Both he and Jenny were safe from his needs tonight.

He closed his eyes and sighed.

Matt lost track of how long they lay together, hearts beating, breaths sighing in and out in unison. The absolute peace of the moment flowed over him like warm maple syrup, melting some of his fears, and his shame.

He'd spent a lot of years living down to his family's reputation. Could he change now?

He didn't know when he'd ever felt so calm. If this wasn't heaven, it was close, lying here in the isolation of the cabin, with rain pounding a steady rhythm on the tin roof and a fire crackling in the hearth, with Jenny in his arms and only two layers of oilcloth and his newfound nobility between them.

He pulled back to look into her eyes, to judge whether she was as affected as he, but they were closed. He nudged her gently, but she didn't move. She'd fallen asleep. He laughed.

After all the drama and tension, she was out like a baby calf without a care in the world. He laughed again and she stirred.

She woke, stared at him with her back to the fire and

her face in shadow. He rolled her over and the firelight set the whiskey highlights of her hazel eyes dancing.

He pulled away from her, because to lie this close to her without making sweet, sweet love was hell.

CHAPTER TEN

MATT KISSED HER forehead once then rolled onto his back.

Jenny turned toward him and he felt her staring at him.

"Have you been to the house since you got back?" she asked. The question came out of nowhere and he stiffened.

She must have sensed it, because she turned onto her side and placed her hand on his chest. Even through the coat, he could feel the weight of it like an anchor. He relaxed slightly and sighed.

"Yeah," he said.

"How was it?"

"Tough." He swallowed and it sounded loud in the room. "There was nothing there for me."

"Nothing?" she asked.

He thought of the mail on the table. "There was an envelope. My parents' autopsy report."

"Oh, Matt." Jenny reached her hand toward his face then dropped it to her side. He knew why. They were already playing with fire, just barely skirting trouble.

"Did you read it?" she asked.

"Mom shot Pop and then killed herself." His fingers spasmed on his stomach. "I already know what happened." He made himself relax. "Why would I want to read the report?"

"What if they found something they weren't expecting?"

"How would that change anything?"

"I don't know. I wonder what they found. I just feel… something."

Before they'd slept together five years ago, Matt had always depended on Jenny to see things about his family he sometimes couldn't figure out on his own.

He remembered the sheer helplessness he'd felt when his parents died. Jenny had anchored him, pure and simple.

"HEY, KID." Deputy Ormstead stood on the veranda, holding his hat in his hand. At least it wasn't Sheriff Saunders, who hated Matt. Matt had opened the door to a knock, already apprehensive. No one visited the Longs. No one *ever* knocked on their door.

When he saw the cop, his first thought was, *I didn't do anything.*

"What do you want?" he asked, his tone belligerent.

The deputy didn't bat an eye, didn't rise to the bait, and Matt felt something shift in him. Had Pop done something? Did Matt need to drag the drunken idiot home from town? How? He'd been driving since he was fourteen, was old enough to drive now that he was sixteen, didn't have the money to get a license.

Shit, what now? Where was Mom? The house had been empty when he got home.

The cop twisted his hat in his hand. He looked nervous. What the hell was going on?

"What?" Matt said, his tone still hard. Whatever it was, Matt wanted him to spit it out and get it over with.

Ormstead took a deep breath. "I have some bad news for you, kid."

"I'm not a kid," Matt said, because he really didn't want to acknowledge the bad-news part and clung to the part that didn't matter.

Ormstead opened his mouth again, hesitated then rushed on. "Your parents are dead."

Matt blinked. What? He didn't know what Ormstead meant. Dead, as in gone for good?

When Matt didn't respond, the deputy repeated it. Matt felt his mouth fall open, suddenly understanding. Couldn't be. No way could Pop die. He was too strong, too fast. He would give death one hell of a chase.

"You okay, kid?"

"Yeah," he said, but his voice cracked.

"Mom's dead, too?"

"Uh-huh." The cop looked as though he'd rather be anywhere but here. "You want someone to come stay with you?"

Yes! "No," Matt said, keeping his voice steady. He didn't want the big man standing in front of him to think he was weak. "I'm okay."

Ormstead nodded and turned away. He walked down the stairs.

Matt needed something, but he didn't know what. Just as Ormstead reached his cruiser, Matt called, "Wait a minute."

The deputy turned back, the hat on his head now and his eyes shadowed.

"What happened?" Matt didn't want to know, but some strange need drove him.

"Your mom caught your dad in the motel with Missy Donovan. She shot him."

Matt sucked in a breath. Yeah, Pop could have given death a run for its money, if not for Mom. He always came back to her—sooner or later—before or after whatever trouble he courted.

"Mom?" he asked, his voice rising.

"She turned the rifle on herself, son."

Matt swayed, had to put a hand on the doorjamb to stay on his feet.

"You sure you don't want someone out here with you?" the deputy asked.

Matt shook his head and focused on a detail.

"How's Missy?"

"She's hysterical, but alive. Your ma didn't touch her."

Matt exhaled. Missy was okay. She wasn't too bright, was too peroxide-blonde and big-chested for her own good, but she was always real nice to Matt.

He nodded. Deputy Ormstead got into his cruiser, slowly, watching Matt. Turning the car in the yard, he still watched him. At the end of the driveway, he stopped, checked Matt in his rearview mirror, gave one hard wave of his hand and drove off.

Matt stood alone on the front porch until he realized he was cold. He must have been standing there for a while. It was a bright September day and the sun shone, but his hands were like icicles. He closed the door and stood in the living room, staring at the unfolded laundry on the table and the margarine and peanut butter open on the kitchen counter and the fireplace full of old ashes.

On the other side of the fireplace, he knew he would find his parents' bedroom a mess. The bathroom would be the same—toothbrushes scattered on the counter, a ring around the toilet bowl, mold between the tiles surrounding the bathtub. Pop's towel on the floor. Matt knew it was there because he'd kicked it out of the way when he got up and had his shower an hour ago. Stupidly, he wondered if that was why Mom shot Pop.

Matt shuddered and fell onto the sofa. This was all his now, every musty bedsheet and all the stale food in the fridge and the ironing board propped in the corner that never, ever got used.

The whole place was his now. The whole kit and caboodle. What did that mean, anyway? Kit? Caboodle? What the hell did it mean? It didn't make sense.

Matt picked up a dirty mug from the scarred coffee table and threw it against the brick fireplace. It shattered into shards of blue and white.

What did it mean?

He picked up another mug and threw it at the fireplace, too. It shattered just like the first.

"What does it mean?" he cried. No one answered—no friend, no family, no God. He dropped to his knees on the floor.

"I don't know what it means," he whispered.

MATT REMEMBERED everything that happened that day—looking out his front window to find Jenny sitting on the big rock in the yard watching the house, with her legs folded under her like a silent guardian angel.

When the reporters came from the larger towns

around, Matt pulled her into the house. Jenny sat on the sofa beside him, for hours and hours, listening to the ringing telephone he wouldn't answer, talking quietly to Kyle and Angus at the door, until he felt strong enough to stand up and phone the one and only funeral home in Ordinary. He made arrangements for the visitation and funeral then sat back down beside Jenny. They didn't say a word to each other, didn't touch, but he felt her presence beside him. She'd steadied him.

MATT JUMPED UP to throw another log on the fire.

Jenny smiled, because she knew he was avoiding the conversation. He knew it, too.

She sniffed the air and laughed. "Take the beans away from the fire. It smells like we burned dinner."

Matt moved the pot.

"There might not be anything new in the autopsy report." She shrugged. "I just feel you need to deal with what happened to your parents."

He lay down alongside her and rested his head on his hand. With his other hand, he picked up a piece of her hair and tickled her nose with it.

She grabbed his wrist and held it still, watched him steadily, daring him to be serious.

"What happened to you was huge. Most people never have to experience anything even half as traumatic as that. You need to deal with it then put it to rest. You need closure."

"I don't go for that kind of psychobabble."

"Anyone would need to deal with his emotions after that kind of ordeal."

He shook his head. "I dealt with it years ago."

"Really?"

"Yeah, really. I got them buried, didn't I? I arranged a funeral service most people came to only because they were curious and scandalized."

"I wasn't."

Yeah, he knew that. She'd shown up at the funeral home two nights running and had stayed until he'd left, trailing him to make sure he got home. Then she'd come to the funeral with a bunch of wildflowers in her hand, picked from the fields and wilting in the heat. She'd clung to those until everyone had left but the two of them. She'd handed him that bouquet of dying flowers and then hugged him.

That gutsy little twelve-year-old, unashamed of either her youth or her premature wisdom, had wrapped her thin arms around his big, sixteen-year-old body, around his anger and shame and insecurity, and had held him until he was just this side of tears. By then, she'd already lost her own parents and knew how he felt. He'd walked away and dumped those flowers in the garbage. Matthew Long, the only son of those two nut jobs in the fresh graves, didn't deserve what she was offering.

He came out of his memory slowly. He'd been staring into the flames and had missed whatever Jenny had said. He looked at her, really looked at her, and realized that he still didn't deserve her. Jenny Sterling had changed over the years. Matthew Long hadn't.

"You're too good for me, Jenny."

He'd startled her. "How can you say that after what I did? I tried to *trap* you into marriage."

"Yeah, you did. That was wrong. But in everything else, you are good and strong."

She looked bemused, as if it confused her to hear a compliment from him.

"Why?" he asked. "Why marry Angus?"

"I want my home back, Matt," she said, her voice full of conviction.

"I remember when it happened," he answered. "When they had the auction on your front lawn."

He needed to do something for her—to comfort her. As much as she sounded confident, her eyes told a different story.

He reached for the buttons of her coat and slipped one out of its hole. He slid the tips of his fingers inside until he felt the soft skin of her belly. She gasped and he kept his fingers still, because he would go too far if he touched more of her.

He remembered how bad he'd felt for the skinny, rough-and-tumble cowgirl who wouldn't let herself cry in public.

She'd sat on the hill overlooking her home, the sorrow and anger seething on her face, yet refusing to give in and cry. Not much more than ten years old and already tough.

He thought about growing up in a home you loved, on land you loved, with parents you loved, and then losing it all. He could finally begin to imagine it. He felt a keen sense of loss for something he'd never had, but had always longed for. Jenny had had it all, and then had been taken away. How must that have felt?

"Is it worth marrying Angus for?" he asked.

Jenny stared at him, swallowed hard, and opened and closed the fist lying on the floor between their heads.

"You want your ranch," he said, his breath stirring her hair. "Angus wants kids. Is that it?"

"It's more than that, deeper than that sounds, but I

don't know if I could describe it well enough to convince you that I'm doing the right thing."

"Angus can't get Kyle back and you can't get your ranch back. Life doesn't work that way, Jenny. Once a thing is gone, it's gone." Her fist clenched on the floor. "We don't get things back. We move forward."

"This *is* moving forward."

"How do you figure that?" His tone had sharpened. "You're selling your body for a house and a piece of land."

She tried to move away from him, but he reached his whole hand inside her coat to rest on her belly and pressed, forcing her to stay and hear him out.

"How is that any different from selling yourself for money?"

She winced at the harshness of the idea. He wouldn't say the ugly words out loud—words like *whoring* and *prostituting*. He would never have thought to see her in those terms and it rattled him.

Awareness filled her eyes and he knew she'd thought of it all herself.

"Don't do it," he pleaded.

"I need to," she whispered. "It's my home. It's what I've always wanted."

"Don't do it," he repeated.

"I have to." There was no softness in her implacable tone. She was going through with it.

In six days, Jenny was going to marry the closest thing to a father figure Matt had ever had. The two people he loved most in the world were marrying each other and it was all wrong. And there wasn't a damn thing he could do about it.

"I need to do this," she said softly.

He grabbed her to him and nestled her back against his front, settling her head on his arm, facing the warmth of the fire. He couldn't fight with her anymore.

"Tell me about it," she said.

"What?"

"Growing up in that house. Do you have any good memories? Or were they all bad?"

He recoiled and tried to move away from her. She held his arm where it was wrapped around her, keeping him there.

"Tell me," she insisted.

Her voice soothed him. Her body curling against him eased his pain.

"Mom used to make pies." Matt smiled. He'd forgotten about that. "When Pop would come home with another rodeo belt buckle, she'd bake a pie—raspberry for first place and apple for second. Not that it mattered. Pop and I loved both."

"So it wasn't all bad?" Her soft voice enticed more happy memories out of him.

"They used to laugh. A long time ago. Early on. In their bedroom late at night."

His throat constricted.

"Matt?"

He told her about the day everything changed, when his mother started to turn into a stranger.

It floated out, the entire memory, and drifted around the room on the heat rising from the fire, told without anger, but as a matter of fact. *This was my childhood.* It just was what it was.

"Do you think we can ever overcome our childhoods?" she asked. "Do you think people have the ability to change profoundly?"

She sounded sleepy.

"I don't know, Jenny. You're asking the wrong person."

Her eyes were half closed, already starting their slide into sleep. She fought it—like a child—forcing them to stay open.

"Tell me more about Wyoming."

"There isn't much to tell," he mumbled.

He felt the moment she lost her battle with sleep. Her body went slack.

He held her close and stared into the fire while she slept, disturbing her only to add wood throughout the night. He couldn't sleep. This would never happen again—Jenny sleeping in his arms as if he had a right to hold her. As if he deserved her.

In spite of having forgiven her, there was still a basic truth that held him back. Jenny had said it about being Jesse's father, but Matt knew it also applied to his relationship with her.

Angus was the better man.

"I'll never marry you, Jenny," he whispered.

She stirred beside him.

She'd heard him.

JENNY AND MATT RODE away from the cabin on the heels of a stunning sunrise. Jenny wanted to hold on to the magic of waking up in Matt's arms as long as she could, but knew there was something she had to discuss with him.

She had enjoyed last night too much. It would never happen again, though. She would only touch him again at work, and that was as it should be. Last night should never have happened. They hadn't shared their bodies, but they had been intimate nonetheless.

Angus deserved better than that, but also, so did she. Matt had made it clear that he would never marry her.

"Matt," Jenny said, her tone resolute.

"Yeah?"

"I'm going to have to ask you to leave the ranch."

He spun his head toward her. "What? Why? Last night won't happen again."

She turned to him with her heart in her eyes. "I'm going to marry Angus on Saturday. It's too hard to have you on the ranch."

His lips thinned. "What about the money I owe Angus? What about Jesse?"

"You can come to the ranch every day to work, but I'll ask Angus to give you your orders."

She directed Lacey into the Circle K yard. Her smile felt infinitely sad. "As far as Jesse goes, I won't keep you from him."

"So I can still work here, I can still see my son, but I can't sleep here."

Jenny nodded. "Yes."

"I can't see how that makes a difference or say that I understand completely."

"Neither do I. It's just something I have to do."

"Okay." He dismounted. "I'll go pack my stuff."

"Matt, come in to breakfast. You can still *be* here, you just can't live here."

Jenny stabled Lacey in the stall next to Master's. She and Matt unsaddled their horses, rubbed them down and left them eating their fill.

They walked across the yard not touching. Remembering his hand on her belly, she regretted that. She wanted to hold his hand, to muss his hair and joke with him, but Angus would always come between them.

They met Angus in the dining room. He sat at the head of the table with a cup of coffee and the newspaper. A flash of relief crossed his face.

He stood and held out a chair for Jenny. "How'd you two do? Find a place to stay?"

Jenny found she was able to greet Angus honestly. She had nothing to hide. True, she and Matt had kissed, but they'd restrained themselves from betraying Angus. And never would betray him in the future. "We stayed in the MacCaffreys' old shack. You?"

"We made it to the MacCaffreys' ranch house. They put us up for the night in the bunkhouse." He sipped his coffee. "Gave us a hot meal, too."

Jenny sniffed. "Something smells good. What did Angela make for breakfast?"

"Buckwheat pancakes."

"You want some, Matt?" she asked, walking toward the kitchen.

"Sure," Matt replied as he watched her cross the room. When he brought his glance back he found Angus regarding him steadily.

The only sound in the room was their breathing.

Matt didn't like what Angus and Jenny were about to do—and couldn't stop them—but he needed to make sure Jenny would be okay.

"I'll take care of her," Angus said, as if he'd read Matt's mind. "You know that."

"Yeah, I know," Matt replied, his hands gripping the back of one of the chairs. Angus would take better care of her than he could.

"She deserves it," he said. But Angus deserved her more.

"I know." Angus refilled his coffee cup from a carafe on the table and picked up the newspaper. "She's a keeper."

She was that, all right, Matt thought, just not his.

Jenny came out of the kitchen with two plates piled high with pancakes. She set one down in front of him, then sat at Angus's place and poured syrup over her pancakes. Matt tried not to watch her, or to remember much of last night. An impossible feat. He would remember every look, every touch until the day he died.

A commotion down the hall caught his attention. Jesse bounded into the room, a big grin on his face.

"Mom! You're home."

Jenny smiled widely and opened her arms. Her son jumped into them and she grunted and said, "Oof," and laughed. He laughed, too.

"Hi, baby. Did you go home with Angela?" Jesse twisted himself around in her arms to face the table.

"Uh-huh. She's got kittens. Can we have one?" He picked up her fork.

"Angela said you were okay. She said you're smart. You'd get out of the storm. Can I have some?" He shoveled a big, adult-size piece of pancake into his mouth, and syrup pooled at the corners of his lips.

"Hi, Matt," he mumbled around a mouthful of food.

"Hey," Jenny said, nudging him. "Don't talk with your mouth full."

Jesse waved to Matt while he chewed. Matt smiled back. The boy was a wonder, full of life and energy, and so loved by his mother it was almost painful to see.

Nothing was going the way it was supposed to. He'd arrived here only a week ago, intent on paying off his debt to Angus and then scooting back out of town, out of Montana, maybe heading north to Canada this time.

But today? Today he was so confused he could barely see straight. One minute he was riding high on the relationship with his son, and in the next minute, he hit bottom in his fear of losing him. Life was unpredictable. Matt didn't want to be anywhere near when any of life's shit hit the fan for his son. Jesse would be better off with a father like Angus to see him through it.

SINCE MATT'S ARRIVAL, Jenny had been on a roller-coaster ride. As much as asking him to leave hurt her, she wanted her quiet life back, just her and Angus and Jesse, with the world on its proper course and them working toward a common goal.

They could get on with the business of marrying and moving forward with the rest of their lives.

How would Matt fit into that now? She just didn't know.

Jenny sighed. Jesse was going to be so disappointed when he realized Matt wasn't staying on the ranch anymore. She had less than a week to get everyone calmed down and focused on the future.

Satisfied that her life was back on the right track, Jenny left the table to tell Angus what she'd done. She really, really hoped he wouldn't blow a gasket.

As usual, she found him in his office, his refuge.

She knocked on the open door. "Can we talk?"

He looked up from the accounts he was working on.

"Sure. What's up?"

"I don't want to upset you, but I've asked Matt to leave the ranch."

Angus didn't look surprised. Why not? Had he noticed her attraction to Matt?

He put down his pen. She had his complete attention. "Where will he go?"

"I don't know. Probably not far. He'll still work here during the day and spend time with Jesse, but he won't be living here."

Angus nodded slowly. She wondered why he didn't ask her how she'd come to the decision, but given that she and Matt had spent the night together, she was afraid he would think the worst.

"Angus, nothing happened last night."

"Never occurred to me that it would. You have a strong set of values."

Maybe, except for what she'd done to Matt.

She twisted her fingers together. "I'm just not comfortable with him here."

"Okay," Angus said. "No problem."

Jenny ran her nail along an indent in the doorjamb. "I'm going to take Jesse over to the Sheltering Arms for the day. I'll stay there, too, for a couple of hours."

She didn't want to watch Matt ride away with his bags packed.

ANGUS SPENT the afternoon on horseback, out on his land. He tried hard to rekindle his pride in his ranch, but his senses had been deadened when Kyle died.

If not for Jenny, he probably would have lost the ranch for all the interest he'd felt in it.

Jenny had got rid of Matt, had sent him off to sleep elsewhere at night. To his shame, Angus was relieved.

He loved Matt, but envied him his son. Angus couldn't even take solace in Matt's presence as the surrogate son he'd once been. He still missed Kyle too much.

Face it, you thought Matt could replace Kyle. It didn't work that way. Even his love for Jesse couldn't fill the terrible void in Angus's soul.

The only time Angus felt anything was when he was with Moira. Those feelings were often in turmoil, anger and pleasure intertwined, but in the middle of the confusion, he felt *alive*.

He spun his horse around and headed back to the house.

The day passed in an endless blur of events to which he felt no connection. Simple things like conferring with Jenny about ranch business, eating lunch and dinner with her and Jesse, checking out a problem with one of the horses.

None of it meant anything. And it had been like this since Kyle's death.

When he was on this ranch, his life was unfocused and gray.

Now Moira was back in town and his moments with her were stunning in their intensity. The grayness of his days became more and more depressing as he got more and more uncertain about the decision he'd made.

The thought of marrying Jenny should bring him joy, but he could see no change in his future other than starting to sleep with Jenny.

That idea left him cold. Jenny was a beautiful young woman, but he didn't love her. Would affection be enough?

He used to think it would be. It might have been had Moira not returned.

But Moira *was* here, she was his one and only, and he panicked at the notion of losing her again by marrying someone else.

Finally, after dinner, he could stand his blue funk and worried thoughts no longer.

He might be on the verge of making a terrible mistake. He needed to talk to Moira.

Minutes later, he was in his car on the road to Ordinary.

He parked in the alley behind Moira's shop and walked around to her door.

The overhead light came on when he knocked. The lace curtain in the window moved.

The door opened.

Moira stood in a satiny pink robe. She stared at him, waited for him to say something.

At this moment, he realized what was about to happen, that the moment he'd left the ranch to drive here, he'd made a decision.

He was desperate and needed more than conversation. He needed the physical warmth with Moira that he'd been missing for too many years.

He opened his mouth. "I can't live the rest of my life with a woman I don't love."

Moira flew into his arms and he held her and closed his eyes. Colors flashed behind his eyelids. He took her head and kissed her, more deeply than he ever had before and she returned his kiss in equal measure.

Her body was lush in his arms, mature and full and perfect. She was sensual and, he hoped, still bawdy after all these years. He meant to find out for sure tonight.

She pulled him into the apartment and turned off

the light above the door. Holding his hand, she led him upstairs, her hips swaying in front of him.

She took him to the bedroom where a small yellow light burned beside a high bed covered with lace and roses.

She drew off her robe and tossed it onto a chair.

The silk nightgown she wore was soft and supple and hugged her generous curves.

He pulled one thin strap off her shoulder to reveal a breast that was more than enough to fill a man's hand. A large brown areola surrounded a dark pink nipple.

Angus bent forward and took it into his mouth and was rewarded with a sigh from Moira.

Her hands scrabbled for his jacket and pushed it from his shoulders, and then reached for the buttons of his shirt, all while he suckled her and she gasped.

In frustration, she tore his shirt open, sending buttons scattering everywhere.

"Angus," she cried, "take off your clothes."

He laughed and obliged her.

"Look at you," she said, rubbing his chest and curling her pink nails through his thick hair. "You've gained weight and muscle. Oh, Angus. You're a man now."

She let her nightgown fall to the floor and lay back on the bed, with her legs open, her only secrets hidden by copper curls.

Yes, she was still bawdy and Angus loved her for that.

He dropped his pants and stood naked in front of her.

She reached for his erection. "Come here. Look at you, my darling."

Angus lay on top of her and loved her. She loved him

back. They used everything at their disposal. Lips and mouths, tongues, fingers and toes.

He'd never thought himself a weak man, never behaved so selfishly, but he needed this night with Moira, to convince himself that giving up his dream of more children was the right thing to do. Judging by how Moira surrendered to temptation, she needed him, too.

She stirred in his arms and released the scent of roses from the rumpled sheets.

He ran his hand over her thigh and around, caressing her full buttock, his fingertips dipping into the crease to fondle the impossibly soft skin where bum meets leg. Running his hand along the back of her thigh, watching her emerald eyes darken, he lifted her leg onto his hip, positioning himself against her.

Her heated aroma rose to greet him, but he stayed where he was, tormenting them both. He knew there was something more she wanted of him than just his body—an answer to the question he read on her face.

When he rested his hand on her chin, his large palm dwarfed her fine jaw. He ran one rough, callused finger across her cheek. "Will you marry me?"

The hope he saw in her eyes turned to joy. "Yes."

She pressed against him.

Her breast overflowed his hand. Yes, this was the right decision.

He suckled her breast, the dark nipple hard on his tongue. She writhed against him.

Dipping lower, he ran his mouth over her round stomach, catching her skin between his teeth, making her gasp, then dipping his tongue into her navel. She moaned and rubbed her generous breast against his shoulder.

He loved every inch of her.

Pulling back, he stared into slumberous eyes and sank into her. He gasped with the sweet ache of her warm welcome.

She was there with him every step of the way. Meeting him thrust for thrust, demand for demand. As if she couldn't get enough of him, of his flesh and his passion, of this union. And he knew how she felt.

He loved her.

Squeezing his eyes shut, he thrust hard and high one last time. Her muscles quivered, draining him dry.

They lay facing each other, sated, and breathed in the heady scent of roses and musk. Moira fell back against the pillow to stare at him.

"In every molecule, I want you. You have all of me. With every particle I will love you."

Angus closed his eyes. His ragged breath fanned copper curls and sent them fluttering around her beautiful face.

He glanced at the clock. Another six hours before he had to return to the ranch and talk to Jenny, to break her heart. He knew what she wanted. And he knew he could no longer give it to her.

CHAPTER ELEVEN

MATT DROVE to his parents' house.

The closest hotel was too far away to do him any good if he was still going to put in full days on Angus's ranch.

Before he'd left the bunkhouse, he'd stripped the blankets from his bed. He had no idea whether anything in that house was worth sleeping on, or whether it was riddled with bugs or mice.

He stepped onto the veranda and stared at the front door, at the green paint peeling, to reveal old white paint underneath. The doorknob had lost any claim to shine years ago.

He raised his hand to push it open, but didn't touch it. Couldn't.

No. He could not, absolutely *not*, sleep in there.

He turned around and strode back to the truck. From the backseat, he retrieved the sleeping bag that he always kept with him. A cowboy just never knew when he would be somewhere where he would need one.

He spread a couple of tarpaulins in the bed, spread out the sleeping bag on top of them and layered the blankets he'd brought on top of that.

He'd forgotten to bring a pillow.

Fully clothed, he slid into his makeshift bed,

pillowing his hands under his head, staring at the light-pricked black blanket above him, picking out the constellations he'd shown his son a few nights ago in the Circle K's yard.

He didn't agree with Jenny's decision that he sleep elsewhere, but he guessed he understood her need to force distance between them.

The wind picked up, whistling through a couple of tall pines behind the house, whispering to him. His loneliness closed around him like a cloak, cooling instead of warming him.

The days of his life stretched before him, with him living a nomadic existence without a home base. He thought of the broken-down house across the clearing. Naw, that could never be home.

Nothing would.

JENNY STEPPED out of the house.

The sun had risen an hour ago and bathed the land with gold.

She breathed deeply of dew-dampened earth and spring grasses.

Angela's yellow crocuses were perky and bright in the sun, her mauve hyacinths fragrant.

Jenny had slept better last night than any night since Matt had returned.

What about those hours in the cabin wrapped in Matt's arms?

Those didn't count. They couldn't mean anything to her. She couldn't let them.

She strode to the bunkhouse and issued the orders for the day. She made a terse statement about Matt sleeping at his own house from now on. There were a few odd looks, but she ignored them. The ranch hands could think whatever they liked. She herself would stay close to the house and spend time with Jesse.

Matt drove into the yard.

She steeled herself to talk to him, to deny the rogue feelings that blinded her when she saw him.

When he climbed out of the truck, he was wearing the same clothes as yesterday. He pulled a bag out of the bed and walked toward her.

"If you don't mind, I still have to shower here."

"Of course, Matt. Do what you need to do."

He looked sullen, but underneath that she sensed real confusion.

"So I can work here and spend time with my son here and eat and shower here, but I can't sleep here. Do I have that right?"

"Matt." A sigh of frustration gusted out of her. "This is just the way it has to be right now. It doesn't make sense to me, either. I just need you to do this for me."

"Fine. Can you ask Angus what my marching orders are for the day? I'll be ready to work in about a quarter hour."

"Eat with the others in the backyard. I'll hunt down Angus and find out what he wants you to do."

Matt headed for the bunkhouse and Jenny to the house to find Angus.

Angela hadn't seen him yet this morning. A pot of coffee sat untouched on the counter. Strange. Angus was usually up long before now and would have consumed a couple of cups.

She checked to make sure he hadn't gone straight to the office.

Turning for the stairs, she tried to remember the last time Angus had slept in past nine.

She checked Jesse. Still asleep.

At the other end of the hall, Angus's bedroom door was open. Strange. He kept it closed when he was sleeping. The bathroom door down the hall was also open. He wasn't in the shower. Jenny stepped inside his bedroom. The bed hadn't been slept in.

Jenny's blood ran cold. Where was he? Where had he spent the night?

She wandered back downstairs. What—?

The sound of a car drew her outside.

Matt stood on the other side of the yard, staring at the approaching vehicle. His face looked flat, neutral, and that in itself was a bad sign. If a friend was driving down the lane, he would be smiling. If an enemy, he'd be angry.

The car pulled into the yard. Angus. But he wasn't alone. The new dressmaker in town, Moira, sat beside him.

Dread started a dance in her chest. No. Please. No.

Moira turned toward her and Jenny saw pity in her eyes. Sadness.

Angus stepped out of the car and stared at her over the roof. His expression of compassion said it all.

There would be no wedding on Saturday, not for Jenny at any rate.

Her head felt as though it would spin off her neck. She grabbed one of the veranda's support columns.

She didn't know where to look. She couldn't stand to face either Moira or Angus. She hated the understanding she felt coming from Matt's eyes.

She badly wanted to run, but didn't know where to go.

The cotoneasters were out of the question. They were too close to the yard and Angus and Moira. To Matt. They held too many of her hopes, too many of her dreams shattered beyond repair.

The screen door opened and Jesse joined her on the veranda. He put his hand on her leg.

"Mom, can I have breakfast?"

She peered at him. The words weren't registering. She had nothing to give to her son at that moment.

Angus approached the steps and said, "I'll take care of him."

"No!" Jenny snapped. She didn't want him near her son. She searched for Matt. Where had he gone?

She grabbed Jesse in her arms and scooted around Angus. He tried to catch her arm. She wouldn't let him, couldn't stand the thought of him touching her, and ran for the bunkhouse.

Matt stepped out of the stable leading Lacey. He had saddled her. He'd known exactly what Jenny would need.

She handed Jesse to Matt and mounted her horse. "Watch him for me."

When she would have ridden off, Matt put a restraining hand on her thigh.

"Run. Get the anger out of your system, but do it safely. Come back in one piece."

His eyes said so much. He understood. He felt bad for her. He was her friend.

She and Matt had resisted each other the night of the storm. It had been one of the toughest nights of her life. Matt had restrained himself when he could have seduced her so easily.

Angus, on the other hand, had spent last night with another woman and Jenny knew they'd done a hell of a lot more than talk.

Who was the better man now? Angus? Or Matt?

She flew out of the yard.

Two hours later, she returned. She wouldn't force Lacey to keep up the pace that Jenny needed to burn off the anger and the terrible, terrible sense of betrayal.

An hour ago, she'd slowed down and had taken her time, riding the ranch that would never, ever be hers again.

When she had finished putting Lacey away, she found Angus sitting on a wicker chair on the veranda.

"Why, Angus?" she asked.

"Thirty-five years ago, Moira and I were in love. We didn't act on it then. I couldn't stand for us to ignore a second chance."

"And last night?"

"Last night, I was weak and I'm not proud of it. I should have broken it off with you first before going to Moira."

"Yes, you should have."

She was drained of all feeling, frozen, wishing that her anger was greater than her shock so she could tell Angus what he and his girlfriend could go do to themselves. And it wouldn't be pretty. Good God, she hated cowards.

Angus's gaze slid away from her. "Jenny, I'm more sorry than I can say. You are a good, good woman. I wish I could be what you need."

"Should Jesse and I move to the bunkhouse?"

Angus stared at her. "Why?"

"Are you going to marry that woman?" Jenny couldn't bring herself to speak her name.

"As soon as possible. Until then, I'll stay in town with Moira. You won't have to see me around here."

"And on your wedding night, will you come back here?"

"I don't know yet. I don't think so. We haven't thought that far ahead."

"Too busy doing other things to talk?" That was low and dirty, but she was only human.

Angus's face flared a deep red. "Jenny—"

She didn't wait to find out what he had to say and entered the house.

What now? Her heart was broken, her life was falling apart, she'd lost her home, and she didn't have a clue what to do next.

THAT NIGHT, as she tucked Jesse into bed, he asked, "So Angus isn't going to be my daddy?"

"No, I'm afraid not."

His lower lip trembled. "Who is?"

"I don't know, honey. Right now, you're stuck with just me."

"If you're not gonna marry Angus, then what about the party?"

"There will still be a party, but it might not be on Saturday night and it won't be for Mommy and Angus. It will be for Angus and a different woman."

"But we can still go, right?"

"Do you want to so badly?"

"Yeah. Mikey says there's going to be lots of pop and

cake." Jenny laughed mirthlessly. The things she never let him eat at home.

That word tripped her up. This was no longer her home. She didn't have one. Neither did Jesse.

"How about if I ask Hank and Amy if you can go to the party and sleep over with Michael?"

"Yeah." That made Jesse happy enough to let Jenny leave him for the night. She heard him settling in as she walked downstairs.

After she phoned Amy to tell her the change of plans and to ask if Jesse could attend the wedding party, whenever that might be, Jenny took a thick sweater out of the closet by the door, wrapped it around her shoulders and stepped outside.

She sat in the aging wicker rocking chair and rocked. And rocked. And rocked.

Around midnight, she knew she should head in to bed.

She did, wondering why she was bothering, knowing full well that she wouldn't sleep.

TWO MORNINGS LATER, with gritty eyes and a sore back from sitting out so long in the chilly air the last couple of nights, Jenny rode the ranch alone.

She didn't know where the ranch hands were or what they were doing. She didn't know where Matt was. She didn't care much about anything today.

Where would she and Jesse go? She'd learned that Angus and Moira were taking a four-day honeymoon after they got married in a couple of days and were then returning to the ranch. Funny, Angus had never offered her a honeymoon.

How could Jenny possibly stay here?

The only good news in a week of bad was that the cattle rustlers had been caught on a ranch on the far side of Ordinary. One less thing to worry about.

The radio crackled. Someone was calling her. It sounded like Matt's voice. She ignored him.

Where would she and Jesse go? The question had rattled around and around her brain for two nights now, and she still had no answer.

The radio crackled again and she turned it off with an impatient flick of her wrist.

Ten minutes later, she heard a horse coming up fast behind her.

Matt rode up. "Something wrong with your radio?"

"Nope."

"Why didn't you answer when I called?"

"Didn't want to."

"We've got a problem along the banks of the creek, in the olive trees."

"You can take care of it."

"I haven't told you yet what the problem is."

"I don't care. Take care of it anyway."

Matt wrapped his fingers around her arm. Where he touched her, he warmed her. She hadn't realized how cold she'd been. Frozen. Dead. His fingers thawed a few square inches of her flesh, but the heat was only skin deep. She wasn't sure what it would take to thaw out her core, but doubted she'd figure it out anytime soon.

"Jenny, you're ranch foreman," Matt said. "Do your job."

She stared out across the fields and felt numb. "Matt, I've worked my ass off for this ranch. When Angus lost his will after Kyle died, I kept it going for him. I cared and cared and cared. For years, I've cared, and it's gotten me nowhere. It got me nothing."

She ambled away. "I don't care anymore."

"Jenny, come with me. Work will help. Come."

He almost sounded as if he was begging. For the first time since he'd ridden up, she looked at him and what she saw would have made her cry if she weren't already so cold and empty.

Dry ice. That's what she was. A big lump of dry ice.

Matt gazed at her with such tenderness, such compassion.

He took Lacey's reins and turned her in the direction he wanted her to go. Then he pressed those reins into Jenny's hand. He laced his fingers through Jenny's other hand and rode along beside her until they reached Still Creek.

MATT DIDN'T LIKE what he saw on Jenny's face, or rather, what he didn't see. She looked dead and that broke his heart. It angered him, but he was afraid to take it out on her.

He wasn't mad at her, but at life. She'd dealt with so much already, and had picked herself up every time, but life had kicked her in the teeth yet again.

"What's the problem?" she asked when they stopped, her voice toneless.

Matt pointed with a coil of rope. "Those steers hiding in the trees. Hip and Kelly moved the herd to another pasture but these guys refused to go. They ran into the trees knowing that neither the men nor their horses would go near those thorns."

"They do that sometimes so they don't have to move.

There must be something in these fields that they like to graze on."

Matt dismounted.

Jenny started to ride toward the trees.

"Stop," he yelled and pulled her out of her saddle. "You know you can't ride in there. Those thorns will tear Lacey's hide apart."

She felt limp in his arms, lifeless, and that worried him.

Her eyes were unfocused. He shook her gently. "Jenny, if you can't care for yourself, at least care for Lacey."

She perked up a little. Maybe he was getting through to her. "Okay." She sounded weary. "What do we have to do?"

Jenny knew better than he did what needed to be done here, but she was clearly lost. Somewhere inside her was the strong Jenny he loved. He just had to coax it out of her.

"I'm going to go in there and wrap the rope around the first steer and then we're going to drag him out. Together. Got it?"

He untied and unrolled his heavy duster from behind his saddle and put it on to protect himself. Those scratches these trees had given him the other day still hurt. He wasn't in the mood for more.

Putting on a pair of sunglasses to protect his eyes, he headed in for the closest steer.

The animal stared at him placidly, chewing on whatever grass or weeds grew under the trees.

He kept chewing while Matt wrapped the rope around his neck. Matt tried to lead him out, but the steer held his ground.

Matt pushed his way backward out of the trees and handed the end of the rope to Jenny. Wrapping his arms around the rope, he said, "Pull."

Nothing happened. "Goddammit, Jenny, pull. I can't do this alone."

She put effort into it this time and they persuaded the steer to come out of the trees.

"One down," Matt said. "Wait here and I'll go back in."

She pulled a little harder with the next and they managed to coax another one out.

Matt dived in four more times and they persuaded every steer but one to come out from among the trees.

The last had a mind of his own. They pulled and pulled until they both let go of the rope at the same time and fell. Matt tried not to land with his full weight on top of Jenny.

He rolled off her as soon as he could.

She started to laugh and laugh. "And people say animals are *dumb*."

"Jenny?" She was hysterical and he didn't know how to help her.

"Jenny," he breathed and held her until her laughter turned to tears. Amazing how sometimes there was so little difference.

"Oh, Matt…" She sobbed against his chest and he thought his heart would break in two.

He held her while the sun beat down on his back. He held her while the steer, still with the rope around his neck, walked out of the trees on its own and started to graze a dozen feet away. He held her until she'd cried herself out.

When she stopped and rolled onto her back, eyes

closed, he took off the duster that had turned into an oven while they had lain on the warm earth.

He spread it out then pulled Jenny back into his arms on top of the coat.

She hiccuped. "Matt," she whispered. "What am I going to do?"

She looked at him with such trust, as if he might have all the answers in the world. Him, a screwup. A coward.

He had no answers for her. He couldn't stand the bleakness in her eyes, though. To make her feel better, he kissed her, gently opening her lips with his tongue and slipping inside.

She stroked the side of his face with her palm, her touch light and tender.

He answered in kind, with soft touches on her face, her neck, the vee of her chest exposed by her shirt.

Unbuttoning it, he caressed her more, over her bra, onto her ribs, across her velvet skin.

He pulled the tails of her blouse out of her jeans, spreading it open.

Unclipping the front closure of her bra, he opened her to the sun. He'd always thought her beautiful, but she'd grown lovelier with maturity.

Her breasts were high and firm, her nipples soft and brown. Eyes still closed, she groped for his hand and brought it to her mouth, where she rested her pursed lips against his palm. Then she placed that moist palm on her breast and her nipple beaded beneath his callused skin.

She draped one arm across her eyes and raised the other above her head, resting it on the grass at the edge of the duster.

She needs me. While Jenny lay still and waited, Matt lifted her breast with his hand and took her hard nipple into his mouth.

He played his tongue over her nipple and on the skin around it, washing her breast with all the comfort he had to give her.

He loved her other breast as well as the first before moving on to her belly.

Lowering the zipper of her jeans, he pulled them down over her hips. A vee of dark hair peeked through the pink lace of her panties. After removing her boots and socks, he slid her jeans off.

Her panties soon joined them in the grass.

She lay in the sun like a goddess. He spread her long, strong legs open and let the sun greet white skin and chestnut hair that had never known its kiss before today.

He ran his lips from the arch of one foot to her ankle, her calf, her knee, her inner thigh, her curls. With his tongue, he parted her and heard her sigh.

He grasped the backs of her thighs and spread her wider, slid his tongue inside her and loved her, gave her all his caring and compassion and tenderness. She poured her response over him, her moisture and her trembling flesh and her need for him.

She whimpered until she came deeply and quietly.

He moved up to lie between her legs and hold her, until her trembling stopped.

"Oh, Matt."

He rose onto his elbows. She moved her arm from across her eyes and the sun turned her hazel flecks to gold. Grasping his head, she kissed him long and fiercely.

His own response was immediate. She reached for his jeans, unzipped them frantically and pulled him out, murmuring, "More."

He pulsed in her hand to the beat of his heart.

He tried to slow her down, sensed her need, gave in and entered her in one stroke.

She was wet and ready and she moved against him like a madwoman. They came together.

He buried his face in her neck, smelled musk and grass.

While she calmed, softened, breathed deeply, he held her, probably for the last time.

He was still the same man he'd always been, not the staying kind that Jenny needed, but while she was here now, his, he would stay and hold her.

Later. He would leave later.

They made love again, with Jenny on top proud and pretty in the sun, whispering nothing more than each other's names. For now, it was enough.

JENNY FELT MATT WITHDRAW, knew the moment he was going to say the things she didn't want to hear.

"Don't," she said.

"Don't what?"

"You know. Don't say whatever it is you have to tell me next. That you can't stay. That you're leaving."

"We both know it's true. We both know it's only a matter of time. Better sooner than later."

She'd known that, but had hoped that in the middle of their magical lovemaking, he had changed.

Her panties lay pink and fragile on the green grass. She pulled them on, then found her bra and covered herself.

Beside her Matt got dressed, too, silently.

When Jenny finished buttoning her blouse, she stood and walked to Lacey, who grazed nearby.

Before she could mount, Matt turned her around and took her into his arms.

It was a goodbye of sorts, and an apology, that he couldn't stay, but that he wasn't yet ready to let her go.

She clung to him. "Thank you," she said softly.

"Don't say that, as if I did you some big favor. You deserve so much more."

He held her face in his hands and whispered fiercely, "You deserve more than me."

She crumpled a bit and then pulled herself together. Matt had given her more than he thought he had. He'd given her strength and comfort for the moment. He'd eased her soul. Had relieved some of the darkness.

"When we get to the house, I'm going to leave. Tell Angus I'll pay him somehow. Take care of our son and love the daylights out of him."

"Matt, don't ever come back. Ever. I can't do this again. I can't keep loving you and losing you."

He nodded.

"If you still want to be Jesse's dad, we'll find a way. But the only reason I ever want to see you again is if you want to marry me. I won't take anything less. Never."

She meant it. Matt wouldn't commit. So she would never see him again.

Tonight, she would mourn. Oh, how she would mourn.

THE FOLLOWING MORNING, after a night of sadness without tears, she mourned hard. The grieving was hell.

Amy had driven over to pick up Jesse for Angus and Moira's wedding. Everyone had decided that, since Hank and Amy had already ordered the food for Angus and Jenny, the wedding would take place that day. Amy knew how awful Jenny would be feeling, so Jenny had the worst time getting her to leave. But she needed to be alone.

The ranch hands had left to attend the celebrations.

The Circle K ranch had never felt so lonely. Well, maybe once, just after her parents had lost it and before Angus and Kyle had moved in.

She couldn't cry, was cried out. She'd gotten rid of her tears yesterday, with Matt's help.

Don't think about Matt and yesterday and the sun on your bare skin.

She knew she would survive. She always did, but she'd lost her anchor.

Loving Jesse would save her. Her love for him would have to be her anchor again, would keep her placing one foot in front of the other every day, would keep her hunting for somewhere else to call home.

MATT CRAWLED out of the sleeping bag and sat up in the bed of his truck, scrubbing his fingers through his hair.

He'd slept badly.

Jenny. Jesse.

He missed them with an intensity that burned. How could he ride out of Ordinary now that he knew about his son? Now that he loved him? How could he leave Montana after what he'd shared with Jenny yesterday?

His heart hurt, ached as if it was going to break in

two. Did hearts really break? Could the human heart recover from this kind of loss?

He wanted his woman. He wanted his son. He wanted his family.

The house mocked him in its run-down drunken glory, as if to say, *What do you know about family? What do you know about love?*

If what he felt wasn't love, he might as well dig his grave now, because he didn't think he could survive this misery.

He thought he'd been lonely after he'd left Jenny five years ago? Ha! This was hell on earth. Why couldn't he learn to stay? Why didn't he deserve what other people had so easily? A normal life.

Enough cowardice.

He jumped from the bed of the truck ready to face down some old demons, his ancient devils.

The front door cried its protest when he pushed it open. He should put a match to it. He should burn down the whole house.

He had only one reason to enter this house for the last time.

He needed answers. He craved whatever might set him free of his legacy. Why couldn't he be his own man, apart from his parents, apart from his past? Apart from the terrified teenager he'd been when he'd gotten Elsa pregnant?

Why couldn't he rise above it all to become a better man? How did he lay his past to rest?

Read the autopsy report, Jenny had said. *You need closure.*

Whatever that meant, he'd give it a shot.

The envelope still lay on the kitchen counter where

he'd left it. He picked it up and slit the top open then carried the report to the table.

His hand trembled when he tried to read the first sheet. He couldn't get past his mother's name. He knew how his parents died. Gunshot wounds. Case closed. He dropped the report.

You need closure, Matt. Jenny's voice again—calm and confident. *What if they found something they didn't expect?*

Okay, he'd make himself read the report. He held his breath while he picked up the document.

Then exhaled loudly when he read the findings.

Dear God. What kind of joke had fate played on his family?

His mother had had a brain tumor. His poor mother had lived with an undetected tumor that had slowly driven her mad. Here it was in hard-edged letters on a crisp white sheet. His mother hadn't had crazy genes. She hadn't passed insanity on to him. The loving mother he remembered from before was his real mother. The older woman had no more control over her actions than a two-year-old would. She had slowly, slowly gone mad, and had been helpless to stop it.

Matt was suddenly furious. What the hell had Pop done about it? Nothing. Not a goddamn thing. Matt remembered her complaints of headaches, and of not feeling well. Pop had let the woman he married lose her mind and hadn't lifted a finger to save her.

He needed to put his demons to rest. He needed to know it all.

Before he left, Matt picked up the framed photograph of him and his mother. In her lucid moments, had she studied it and wondered where she had gone? Why she was no longer the woman in the photograph?

He drove into Ordinary, to visit Missy Donovan.

Missy lived in a small, neat bungalow on the far side of town. She'd had a gentleman friend who'd set her up in this house and had furnished it for her. He'd taken care of her until his death five years ago. Matt wondered how she got by now.

Rosebushes lined the path to her front door. A wicker chair sat on the whistle-clean veranda, pure white with a green cushion.

A brass knocker in the shape of a cat gleamed on the front door. Matt rapped it against the wood.

Missy answered, her eyes widening when she saw him. She nodded, then said, "I thought you might show up eventually. C'mon in."

She led him into a small, neat living room. She gestured to the sofa. "Have a seat."

Matt was glad to see Missy no longer dyed her hair. It had changed back to black, streaked with gray. It curled softly around her face, making her look younger than the long, blond stuff had. She'd gained weight in middle age, but she still looked good. She always did have half the men in town panting after her like bloodhounds. Everyone said she was easy. He didn't know about that.

"You want an iced tea?" she asked.

He nodded. "Thanks."

She didn't ask why he was here.

Matt studied the room when she went to the kitchen. The furniture wasn't the best, but neither was it cheap. She'd got herself a cozy little setup out of her last man.

A photo of a stunning young woman caught his eye.

She looked familiar. He stood and walked to the mantel, studying the picture with every step. The woman looked out at the world with a sensuality that rivaled Missy's, but with more confidence and in-your-eyes bravado. This was a woman who made dares—and never turned one down.

The black of her hair gleamed with the healthy sheen of youth, and matched the eyebrows above her brilliant blue eyes.

"That's my Angel," Missy said behind him.

"This is little Angel?" He looked at Missy over his shoulder. He vaguely remembered Missy's daughter—a child just passing into adolescence when he'd left town. "She's grown up real well. She's a stunner."

Missy smiled. "She's nineteen and a lot prettier than I ever was."

"That's not true. She got her looks from you."

Missy laughed. "Your father was a charmer, too." She saw Matt's face tighten and said, "He could be kind."

Not likely. Not his father.

She put his glass of tea on the coffee table in front of the sofa then sat in the armchair and reached for her cigarettes. She lit one and her bosom rose and fell as she drew on it.

The cancer society oughta shoot Missy Donovan, Matt thought. She was the only woman he'd ever known who made smoking look sexy. On everyone else, it looked cheap and tough. Missy had a sensuality a man could lose himself in. Was that what Pop had done? Matt felt bad for his mother. How could she fight what Missy had to offer, with half of her brain already eaten by a tumor?

"He loved her, you know." Missy must have been a

mind reader. "Your father was crazy about your mother until the day she killed them both."

She sucked on her cigarette again with those beautiful lips then blew smoke through the small perfect circle they made.

"I saw your father off and on for years." When she read the disapproval on Matt's face, Missy continued, "I don't say this to hurt your feelings. I want you to know the man your father really was. I'm pretty sure you didn't see much of the good in him when you were growing up."

She cleared the huskiness out of her throat. "He came to me for sex. That was it. What he and your mom had the last few years was too wild for him, but he couldn't stop going back for more."

This was way too much information. Matt didn't want to know any more about his parents' sexual relationship than he already did.

"He came to me for boring, plain, dull, ordinary sex."

Matt frowned. He couldn't imagine that of Pop, or of the sensual creature sitting across from him.

"Trust me. He gave his passion to Gloria. He brought his physical needs to me." She took a final puff on her cigarette then squashed it in a small crystal ashtray. "And we talked. We'd make love once each night, then we'd talk for the rest of the night—about Gloria and how much he missed the woman he married."

Matt felt the anger rise in him again, that Pop had done nothing to help Mom. "Why didn't he take her to a doctor? Why didn't he help her?"

"He took her to a shrink who gave her medication

that made her a vegetable. He couldn't stand it. Neither could she. She threw the pills away."

Matt gripped the arm of the sofa. "Couldn't he have done something else?"

"He didn't have a clue what else to do. He was so mad at her for going crazy, but he could see the hurt and frustration in her eyes. He got so angry whenever he saw her."

"Tell me about it," Matt muttered.

"He had to booze himself up just to go home and then he'd come back to me, crying."

"Pop? *Crying?*" Matt shook his head. "No way."

"Yes," Missy said in her calm, husky voice. "Crying. He missed her, Matt. He missed the real woman inside."

So did Matt. He put his hand over his heart, where it ached for missed opportunities, for what-might-have-beens if his mother had never developed that tumor.

"Your father just wasn't mature enough, or sophisticated enough, to deal with it. It killed him in the end."

"She had a tumor," he said.

"Oh, Lord. Was that what made her crazy?"

Matt told Missy about the autopsy report.

"That's tragic. So sad for all of you."

"Did you know my mother?" he asked, starving for the parts of her he only hazily remembered. He hungered for details about her.

"Your father married her and brought her home from a rodeo in California. He boasted that he came back with two trophies, a belt buckle and your mother."

Matt smiled. He could imagine Pop doing that, showing Mom off in her young prettiness.

"She was a waitress in a bar. Had a lovely smile. Used to sing a bit, too." Missy seemed lost in her memories.

"Keith never came into town without Rose on his arm." Missy's smile was tinged with envy. "They were glued to each other. Madly in love. No wonder. Rose sure was a knockout. Friendly, too."

Matt drank it in, ate up all the details of the woman he remembered in feelings, inside, if not in actual memory.

"What happened to them later was a real shame," she said.

When she lit another cigarette, a gold wedding band glinted on her finger.

"Hal married me before he died," she said, answering his curious look. "Only time I've ever been married. It lasted twenty-four hours. He died the next day."

"I'm real sorry about that."

She shrugged. "We had two years to prepare for it. We made good use of those years." Her lips curved into a soft smile and Matt was glad she had happy memories.

"What did he die of?" he asked.

"Cancer. I nursed him."

Matt nodded. Yeah, she was the kind of woman who would stick with a man to the end.

When the iced tea and memories were spent, Matt stood to leave.

"There's something else you need to know before you go," Missy said.

"What's that?"

She pointed to her daughter's photograph. "Angel is your half sister."

CHAPTER TWELVE

HE HAD A SISTER.

Matt couldn't get his head around that. His dad and Missy had made a sibling for him and he'd never known. All those years when he'd felt so alone, he'd had a little sister in town. So close. He could have gotten to know her. Could have cared for her the way older brothers do with baby sisters.

He sat in his pickup truck outside Missy's house, still stunned by her announcement.

Matt needed to see Angel, to talk to her, to find out what she thought about having a brother, but she was away in Bozeman attending Montana State University. Missy was proud of Angel, with good reason. With Missy's poor background, she'd probably never thought a child of hers would continue her education after high school. Thanks to Hal's money and to Missy's nursing him in his last years, Angel had a chance to move ahead in life.

Hal had done better by Angel than her natural father had. Did Angel even know about Keith Long? So many questions needed answering. Missy promised to contact him the next time Angel came home for a visit. He couldn't wait to see her.

Matt thought about his parents.

One lousy, lousy twist of fate had screwed up his

parents and their marriage and, as a consequence, him. Matt wanted to howl at the savage injustice of it.

He would never end up like his mother. If he ever got her symptoms, he would know what was wrong. He'd have them check for a tumor.

He wasn't his father, either. Except for that one mistake with Elsa and the terror of the depth of his love for Jenny, he'd been responsible. Matt had sown a few wild oats, had made a bit a money on the rodeo circuit, but he hadn't spent ninety percent of his life chasing belt buckles, booze and women. He'd also been a hard worker.

He would never die from a shotgun blast.

Was he enough like his father to abandon his son? No!

He refused to be his dad, or to act like him. He was the one Long father who was going to break the mold and raise his child with reliability and a whole *shitload* of love.

Matt had been alone for so many years. He wasn't alone anymore.

A couple of weeks ago he'd had nobody. Now he had a son and a half sister he'd never known about. His heart swelled with the knowledge that it mattered to him. It *all* mattered—having a family. Keeping a family.

Keeping Jenny.

He wanted her with an ache that left him breathless. He wanted her for all eternity. He wanted to make a family with her.

When Angel returned to town, he would get to know her. And he'd get to know his son even more than he already had.

There was no comparison between his relationship

with Jesse and what he'd had with his own father. Already Matt felt he was doing a better job.

He'd go to Jenny and marry her. He'd treat her and Jesse with all the tenderness and love they deserved, because some weird twist of fate could screw it up. He was tired of living a buggered-up, lonely life. He was stronger than his poor, lost man-child of a father.

Whatever problems he encountered, he was capable of dealing with.

He was going to grab hold of his family and hang on tight, and stay through everything.

Matt needed Jenny. Now. Yesterday. Tomorrow. Forever.

He was going to marry her.

Jenny Sterling, my pure, steady guardian angel, I'm coming to get you.

"Thanks for the tea," he called as he waved out the window and drove away from Missy Donovan's house. He needed his family. He needed his son and the woman he loved.

He had no idea where they were going to live, or how they would support themselves, but they were going to be together.

TWENTY MINUTES LATER, Matt arrived at the Circle K. The place was empty. Of course. The wedding was today.

Jenny wouldn't have gone. He ran into the stable. Lacey was in her stall.

He went into the house and called her name. No answer.

Just about ready to check the top of the hill, he had a thought.

Had she slept as badly as he had last night?

He took the stairs two at a time.

She lay on top of her bed in a T-shirt and panties. Her jeans lay on the floor where she'd dropped them when she went to bed.

She'd left her socks on. One of them was half off, making her foot look twelve inches long.

He smiled. Lord, he loved everything about her.

Nudging her, he lay down beside her. She moved in her sleep, rolling halfway over.

Starting with her foot, he touched her, ran his hand up her leg, skirted the apex of her thighs and rested his hand on her stomach.

Her skin felt soft enough to sink into.

He leaned up on one elbow to watch her wake and moved his hand once more, to her breast. No bra.

She came awake gradually, with a tiny purring sound in her throat. He'd always known this about his tomboy—that she was a sensual creature.

Jenny opened her eyes slowly.

"Dreaming?" she whispered.

"No."

She closed her eyes again, and moaned in what sounded like pain. He'd done that to her, to this woman who was too strong to break. He'd wounded her. No more.

Her body reacted to him, her nipple beading against the fingers that played with it.

"I can't say no to you," she said. "I thought I was strong, but I'm not."

He kissed her temple and tasted salt on his lips. "You are strong, the strongest person I know."

His hand roved to her other breast.

"I can't be strong when you're touching me."

"I'm making a commitment," Matt said.

A furrow appeared between Jenny's eyebrows. She didn't understand. Or was afraid to believe him. He was suddenly desperate. If he couldn't explain in words, he'd find another way to show her. Heat smoldered in his body. He needed her. He pulled off his shirt and threw it onto the floor with her jeans. She stared at his chest.

He lay down beside her again, still circling her breast with his fingers. His erection strained against his pants, but he refused to rush. He had all the time in the world. He held her gently but firmly, not wanting to hurt her, but not wanting to let her go either. This, *this,* was heaven, holding Jenny.

She turned around in his arms, color high on her cheeks.

"What did you say?"

"I'm making a commitment. I want to marry you."

She stared at him. "Really?"

"Really. As soon as possible."

"Why— How?" Her warm breath fanned his face.

"Shh. Later. For now, just enjoy."

Matt reined himself in, forced himself to go slowly, to lick her from breasts to navel with a measured intensity that inflamed them both. Jenny writhed beneath him, and let out small moans that heated him with tenderness, made him search harder for the spots that would entice more of those delicious sounds from her.

He needed to see more of her and pulled back.

Jenny watched him silently, solemnly, her hands on his shoulders, her body long and lithe, and bathed in soft light filtered by lace curtains on the window.

He slipped one finger under the fragile thong strap riding high on her hip and dragged her panties down her legs.

He spread her legs and stared at the treasure there, protected by curls dark against the intimate flesh.

"Jenny." He breathed her name like a benediction, knowing how it would warm her. She shivered and waited for his next move.

He pressed his lips to the soft curls.

Her heat rose to greet him. Her legs widened to welcome him. He explored. Licked. Stroked. Dampened. Tasted. Cradling her tush in his palms, he lifted her to him to delve more deeply into her wet core, getting drunk on her essence.

She writhed and pushed herself against his ravening mouth. He gave everything he had with the sweet hope that it would be enough. She keened high and softly, and he wanted to swallow that sound. She stiffened and wrapped her thighs around him to hold him still.

Her lush scent sent him reeling with need.

She dropped to the bed with a long sigh that sounded like his name. He smiled, saw his future full of endless nights of loving Jenny.

He sat back on his heels and stared at the long, hot vision in front of him, a muscled, sleek cat of a woman who stretched sinuously. Then she opened her eyes, dark with passion and satisfaction.

She rose to sit in front of him, to lean in and kiss him. He closed his eyes, felt the tip of her tongue against his lips, knew that she would taste herself there.

Jenny opened her mouth on his and became bold, holding his face between her hands while she explored him, pulled away with slow luxury before pushing him onto his back. She straddled him, sitting on his erection, which strained for release from his jeans, and moved her hips in circles of exquisite torture.

She threw her head back, leaving her neck long and bare above her gently swaying breasts. Her hips undulated. Her stomach tightened and eased with each luscious circle. The bare flesh of her upper thighs gripped his hips.

Matt groaned. He could watch her for all eternity.

Sweet Jenny.

Devouring him with the eyes of a hungry woman, she leaned forward, raised his arms above his head and pressed them into the bed. Then, with wonderfully slow strokes, explored his biceps and shoulders and chest and his sensitive heaving abdomen with her capable hands, leaving a trail of heat as potent as the Montana sun.

Those hands unzipped the denim and touched his flesh and he gasped. He felt the wonderment in her, in the way she cradled him with tenderness that suddenly changed to conviction to urgency to a wet hot tight Jenny welcome thank you thank you thank you.

He hissed.

She gripped him hard and tight, moved muscles, spectacular flesh, pretty breasts. Yes, love. Yes, Jenny.

He stiffened, held her hips still, came and shivered.

This woman.

Jenny.

He pulled her down onto him, held her against him while their hearts hammered in their chests. He shoved his fingers into her hair and ravished her mouth, pouring himself into her until he fell back, spent, against the lace comforter.

He stroked her skin and held her beautiful behind in his hands.

"I love you, Jenny."

She lifted her head and met his gaze with sleepy eyes.

"I love you, Matt," she whispered, her voice deep and womanly.

He stroked her cheek with one finger then placed his hand back on her behind.

"My beautiful, true Jenny."

She rested her head on his chest. The satin of her hair brushed his sensitized skin.

He sighed.

Matt awoke to a dim room, lit only by the soft grays and purples of dusk, with Jenny still on his chest, asleep, his hands on her bum. He grinned. Life was good.

He wrapped his arms around her and squeezed. He would be true to this woman for the rest of his life. Nothing and no one would come between them.

She stirred and moaned.

"Oh, my legs," she murmured. "Oooh, my thighs."

He tapped her lightly on the rump. "You should be used to it with all the horseback riding you do."

Jenny sat up and looked down at him with sparkling eyes. "I will never, ever get enough of this."

He grinned. "We're going to try, darling. We're going to spend the rest of our lives trying."

He lifted her off him and threw her onto the bed on her back. She laughed and he got high on the sound.

He kissed her stiff thighs to make them better.

She laughed again, lighting the room with her joy.

God, he loved her.

He jumped off the bed and hooted, loud and long. He drew her off the bed and into his arms.

"If I wasn't so hungry, I'd stay here and love the daylights out of you. Let's go downstairs before I give in."

Jenny took a plaid shirt out of her closet.

Matt rummaged through the bedsheets for her panties.

He searched the covers and the floor, then got down on his knees and found them under the bed.

"How the hell did they get under there?" He threw them to her.

She grinned and pulled them up her long, long legs. Matt nearly lost it, nearly dragged her back to bed. He turned around, got himself dressed and ran out of the room.

"I'll see you in the kitchen," he called as he hustled down the stairs. "Hurry! I'm an impatient man. I need to eat and then get right back up here."

"Why here?" she asked. "There's a great fireplace in the living room."

He smiled then sauntered to the kitchen. He was going to enjoy being married to Jenny.

The world was finally irrevocably right.

THEY ATE LEFTOVER lasagna beside the fire that Jenny had built.

"You make a good fire," Matt said. "In more ways than one."

He leaned toward her and kissed her.

With his eyes so close, so blue, Jenny asked, "Is this real, Matt?"

"More real than anything I've ever done."

"When you left this last time I thought I'd never see you again. What happened?"

"I've been sleeping in the bed of my pickup. When I—"

Jenny cut him off. "In your truck?"

"Yeah. I couldn't sleep in that house."

"I just assumed you would. If it's any consolation now, I'm sorry. I know I was being irrational." She kissed him before continuing. "I was terrified that I wouldn't be able to resist you, that I would haul you out of your bed one night and drag you into mine."

"For the record, I don't believe you would have done that. You are so strong, Jenny."

When she would have argued, he said, "Moving on, I woke up miserable this morning. I felt like my life was over. I couldn't stand the pain of losing you and Jesse."

Matt stared into the flames. Jenny waited for him to continue. She knew that *he* thought he was sure of his change of heart, but *she* had to hear it herself.

"I kept asking myself why I couldn't have you and Jesse, why I didn't deserve to live a normal, happy life. So I went into the house and read the autopsy report."

That startled Jenny. "Matt, that was brave of you."

"I was shaking the whole time. Imagine that, a grown man shaking because of a few scraps of paper."

When he looked at her, there was wonder in his eyes. "She wasn't insane, Jenny. Mom had a brain tumor."

Jenny covered her mouth with her hands. "A tumor?" All those years lost because of that. Three lives ruined by a mass of deadly tissue.

"Yeah," Matt said. "No weird genetics. No crazy DNA. I'll never end up like her." He wrapped his hand around the back of her neck and urged her forward. He kissed her lips. "And Pop was just a weak man. I won't be that weak again, Jenny. I promise."

She could see in his face his absolute belief that he would never again be his father, he would never be the young man who ran away when the heat became too much.

He had grown. In his eyes, she saw conviction and a new maturity.

Jenny suddenly felt weepy. So many tears in the past had been hidden or buried because of pride or the fear that she might never stop crying, but these? These were happy tears burning the backs of her eyelids.

"This is real, isn't it?"

"You'd better believe it, Jenny. We're getting married and we'll stay that way forever."

Oh, oh, the sweetness.

Jenny took Matt's plate and set it aside on top of her own, then pushed Matt onto his back. This time she was the aggressor.

Too much happiness and love roiled inside of her to put into words, so she put it all into action, telling him exactly how she felt.

THE FOLLOWING MORNING, Jenny woke up sprawled with Matt in front of a cold fireplace. Sometime during the night they'd decided to sleep here.

She'd spread blankets on the floor and had brought down her lace comforter from her bedroom.

Snuggling under it against Matt's side, she counted her blessings. Jesse. Matt. They had no place to live, but that was okay.

Before falling asleep in Matt's arms, Jenny had

realized that home wasn't a piece of land or a ranch house. Her home had a pair of names—Jesse and Matt.

They could live anywhere and her love for them would be as powerful as the love she'd shared with her parents in this house, and would be more potent than her love for this land.

The fire had gone out hours ago. No matter. They'd made good use of the fire throughout the night.

They seemed to have a penchant for making love in front of fires. Jenny vowed to make sure it happened often throughout their lives.

Matt stirred beside her.

She heard his morning-husky voice say, "Good morning," and felt it rumble through the hard chest under her ear.

"Good morning." She looked up at Matt and smiled. "The best morning ever."

"It's chilly in here."

Jenny stated the obvious. "The fire died."

While he unfolded his beautiful body and shoved aside the screen, he said, "I'll build it back up."

"We don't need it. It's time for breakfast."

Matt squatted in front of the grate with kindling in his hand and peered at her.

"Yes, Jenny, we *do* need a fire."

The banked fire in his eyes set parts of her body tingling. She saw his desire for her, but it was different than it had ever been before, uncomplicated and clean.

His love for her was unmarred by the past or someone else's sins. Matt was his own man now.

Under his talented fingers, the fire leaped to life. Flickering flames lovingly kissed the hills and valleys of Matt's strong body. Lean and muscular, Matt was Jenny's perfect man.

She had a right to touch this body from now on, without fear or shame. Matt was hers.

He watched her over his shoulder. If she had the right to stare at Matt's beautiful body, he had the same right with hers.

She pulled the comforter away from her body and let him look his fill.

Too quickly, her body cooled and she shivered.

Matt covered her from head to toe with his solid heavy body and she'd never felt so warm or so safe.

They loved each other with a thoroughness that left them trembling.

Afterward they lay boneless. Everything in the world was so right.

Jenny's happiness threatened to overwhelm her, so she said, "Let's go get Jesse and tell him about his daddy. He's at the Sheltering Arms. Let's share our news with Hank and Amy, too."

They ran upstairs to shower, but that took a while. Matt didn't think Jenny was quite clean enough and had to wash her pretty thoroughly after she'd already finished scrubbing herself.

Her giggles rang around the bathroom, echoing against the tiles in the shower stall and punctuated by Matt's deep laughter.

Eventually, finally, they finished and dressed, but Jenny wanted tonight to be here *now*.

They rode over to the Sheltering Arms because it would take longer than driving and held hands all the way, while Lacey and Master bumped up against each other. The horses also grazed every time Matt stopped to kiss Jenny, or she stopped to kiss him.

Jenny smiled because she thought she could almost hear their thoughts.

Enough already.

Nope. Jenny sighed. The rest of her life would not be enough. She planned to love Matt well and often.

They rode into the Sheltering Arms Ranch and heard children's laughter floating from the stable. They dismounted and left the horses tied to the corral fence.

Hand in hand, they followed the sounds of that laughter. Jenny's heart raced. Wait until Jesse heard.

She saw Hank first.

"How was the party?" she asked.

Hank stared at them as if he'd never met them before. Most particularly, he stared at their joined hands.

Jenny grinned. "We have good news."

Hank didn't wait to hear what it was because it had to be so clearly written on her face. He hauled Jenny up into an embrace that could rival an Angus Kinsey hug. A split second after he dropped her to her feet, he grabbed Matt and hugged him, slapped his back, shook his hand.

Since marrying Amy, Hank loved anything to do with marriages and happily-ever-afters.

Jenny couldn't wipe the grin from her face. Her muscles refused to obey.

"Where's Jesse?"

"Jess!" Hank hollered.

Jesse came down the aisle, jumping over beams of sunlight where they fell through small cracks in the wall.

When he saw Matt and Jenny he squealed, "Mom! Matt!" and he threw himself against their legs.

"Michael, Cheryl," Hank called. "We're heading inside." To Matt and Jenny, he said, "Let's go share this with Amy."

Amy shrieked when she heard and hugged Jenny and kissed Matt soundly on the mouth.

"Where is the wedding?" she asked.

"We haven't even talked about that." Jenny had no idea where their future lay, whether they could find a place near Ordinary for themselves.

When she mentioned this, Hank asked, "The Long land?"

Matt shook his head. Knowing the reasons for his past unhappiness didn't erase the bad memories.

"How about here?" he asked. "We can find some-place for you to settle in."

"Hank, thank you, but we need a place of our own." She didn't know whether Matt agreed until he caught her eye and nodded.

Two hours later, they left the Sheltering Arms on horseback. Jesse rode on Matt's lap. The picture they made warmed Jenny to the tips of her toes.

CHAPTER THIRTEEN

ANGUS AND MOIRA returned Thursday from their mini-honeymoon. As they drove down the laneway to the house, Angus was nervous. He didn't know what to expect. How was Jenny going to feel about him? About Moira?

Would she even still be here?

He stepped onto the veranda just as Jenny came to the front door.

A soft smile lit her face, untainted by anger. Why?

"What happened?" he asked. "The last time I saw you, you were furious with me. You looked like you never wanted to see me again."

"I was, yes. I can't agree with your methods, Angus, but you were right. We didn't love each other. Getting married would have been a mistake."

Angus's fear evaporated. "Thank God. I thought I'd lost your friendship."

Jenny's expression sobered. "You have lost some of my respect, but I'd like to find that again. You were always good to me, Angus."

He opened his arms and Jenny walked into his hug.

"I'll miss your Angus Kinsey hugs," she said.

"Hey, I'll make sure Moira understands that they're available to you whenever you need one."

"I'd like that, Angus." She seemed to turn shy. "I might not need them, though."

That saddened him. He had deep affection and respect for Jenny.

"I have good news of my own."

He smiled. "What's that?"

"Matt and I are getting married."

Angus let out a shout of laughter. "That's wonderful! How did this come about?"

"Come," Jenny said. "Let's sit over here."

"I'll tell Moira to join us. She was too worried to get out of the car."

"Wait, Angus. I'd like to talk to you alone first. It'll be hard for me to accept her. What you two did was pretty rotten."

Angus's collar suddenly seemed too tight. "Jenny, I'll regret what I did to you for the rest of my life. I should have handled the situation better."

"Yes, you should have. I care for you, Angus. Because of the good times we've shared, it's easier for me to forgive you than Moira. She knew we were engaged and she slept with you anyway. The least she could have done was to send you home to break things off with me first."

Jenny brushed a lock of hair from her face and held it while the breeze tried to move it again. "I have no relationship with this woman, no happy past, but I will try to like her and to forgive her. For your sake, if nothing else. No guarantees, though."

"I understand." Angus covered her hand with his and squeezed. "If you're willing to try, that's enough for me."

He turned and gestured for Moira to join them.

Angus couldn't watch Moira step out of the car and mount the veranda steps without feeling his heart swell. He'd been given a second chance at love and was holding on to it with both hands.

Moira stood in front of Jenny hesitantly. Strange for her to hesitate about anything. Then Angus realized that she wanted Jenny to like her and his heart swelled even more.

"You two have never officially met," he said. "Moira, this is my special friend, Jenny."

Moira smiled and extended her hand. "Jenny, I want to apologize for my behavior. I wronged you and I'm sorry."

Jenny's expression was cool, but she unbent enough to shake Moira's hand.

"Jenny and Matt are getting married," Angus said and Moira smiled.

"I'm so glad," she said.

Angus directed them all to the wicker chairs. "Tell me," he said to Jenny.

She related what had happened while he and Moira had been gone.

Angus laughed. "Where's Matt? I want to congratulate him."

"He's out looking for a place for us to live."

That surprised Angus. "But why not here?"

Jenny leaned forward. "I don't think that would work, Angus."

"Why not? You could stay on as foreman. Matt could continue to work here."

"Where would Jesse and I sleep? In the bunkhouse with Matt?"

"You could stay in the house. It's large enough."

"Not for two sets of newlyweds."

"She's right, Angus," Moira said, laying a gentle hand on his knee. "We all need our privacy. Jenny will have a family. She should have a place of her own."

"Has Matt had any luck?" Angus asked.

Jenny shook her head. "There's nothing available these days."

Angus knew what the answer would be but asked the question anyway. "Matt's house?"

Jenny shook her head harder. "Too many bad memories. He'd just as soon burn the place down."

"I can't say I would feel differently if I was him."

"Apparently, when he first came back, Matt put the ranch up for sale. He only changed his mind after I told him about Jesse. Then he decided the land could be Jesse's legacy. But the house? No. Matt doesn't want Jesse in there. Ever."

The breeze kicked up the scent of lilacs.

"Matt's going to try to sell it again. Paula Leger and her father are searching for properties, but it looks like we may have to move a fair distance away to get something we can afford."

Angus's heart dropped into his boots. He knew that Matt could never replace Kyle, but he sure felt like a son to Angus anyway. He wanted Matt nearby.

His affection for Jenny was genuine and strong. He would love to start thinking of her as a daughter, which meant he didn't want to see her leave, either.

And Jesse? Jesse made him feel alive. It was good to have someone young in the house after so many years without children around. And now Angus might lose them all.

"Where's Jesse?" He rose out of his seat. He needed to see the little guy.

"In the kitchen with Angela," Jenny said.

Angus moved to the door and called into the house, "Jesse."

He heard a scream of delight and then Jesse was running down the hall and jumping into his open arms.

Angus clasped him to his chest. The small bundle smelled like vanilla and chocolate.

"You been baking?" he asked.

Jesse nodded so hard flour drifted from his hair onto his shirt. Onto Angus's, too.

Oh, Lord, he would miss this child.

"Come out here." He carried Jesse to the women and sat down, settling Jesse onto his lap. "I want you to meet someone."

Angus took Moira's hand in his. "This is my new wife. Her name is Moira."

"I meeted Mora already."

Angus pushed his eyebrows up high for Jesse's benefit. "You did? I didn't see you at the wedding."

"I was there! Mommy couldn't come so I went and stayed with Mikey. Mommy stayed here. Matt did, too."

Angus's brows rose for real this time. "Really?"

He glanced at Jenny and her cheeks flushed. He started to laugh.

"Well, well, well," Angus said. "So *that's* how the engagement came about."

Jenny shrugged and looked away, but those cheeks stayed pink.

Angus was grateful that Jenny was still his friend.

Angela stepped out of the house with coffee and warm cookies.

Jesse took one and bit into it. He twisted around in Angus's lap to look at him and told him about what he'd done since Saturday.

Angus's heart melted at the normalcy of the scene. He loved this boy dearly. He wanted him close. And Jenny. And Matt.

Later, after he'd carried his luggage up to his room and he and Moira had sorted out where her clothes would go, Angus looked around and said, "This isn't half as pretty as your room is."

"Can I change it?"

"Yes."

"Are you sure you wouldn't mind?"

Angus grinned. "Not at all. I've grown fond of flowery sheets and the scent of roses."

He kissed his wife and their tongues danced.

Angus wrapped his arms around her and sighed. "I love you. I'm so glad you're here."

Moira pulled back to look at him. "You'll miss Matt and Jenny and Jesse, won't you?" Her eyes held an understanding he didn't expect to see there. They'd been apart for so many years yet she knew him well.

"I will. They mean a lot to me."

Angus stepped away. While he'd been unpacking, a wild idea had been running through his head. "Would you mind taking a drive with me?"

"Of course not."

Minutes later, they were out on the small highway that led to Ordinary.

Angus turned off at a narrow road and drove through a tunnel of overgrown lilacs.

"Those need to be pruned," Moira said. "They don't have as many blossoms as yours do."

"You noticed that already?"

"I noticed a lot of things about your ranch while I was waiting for you to talk to Jenny."

She shifted to watch him navigate the rough dirt road. "You did well for yourself over the years, Angus."

Her pride in him felt good.

"I want you to keep an open mind about this place until I can explain some things to you. Okay?"

"Okay."

The road opened into a clearing where the most run-down house this side of Billings listed in the sun and seemed about to fold in on itself.

"What is this place?" Moira asked.

"This is where Matt grew up." Angus told her as much as he knew about Matt's upbringing as well as the stuff he'd suspected. "I'm pretty sure Matt never wants to set foot here again."

He leaned across her to get a better look at the property.

"I want you to ignore the house and just look at the land."

They stepped out of the car. Moira turned full circle.

"Those lilacs would be beautiful if they were in bloom. And those pines around the back are stunning."

She touched the big rock in the centre of the clearing in the front yard. "I would plant perennials around this and surround those with a lawn."

She peered around. "This is a lovely, lovely piece of land. I see a lot of potential here."

She met his gaze. "I could certainly live here, but not—" she pointed to the old house and finished emphatically "—in *that*."

Angus smiled. Oh, yeah, she understood him well. "Are you thinking what I'm thinking?"

"Yes."

"Good. Let's go tell the kids."

MATT SAT at the kitchen table, so damn discouraged. There were plenty of foreclosures in northern Montana, but all big ranches, nothing that they could afford even at those bargain prices.

He'd checked out one cheaper place, but it had made his parents' house look good.

Jenny sat across from him, picking at her lunch desultorily.

"There's no way around it," he said. "I have to get a job and save up a down payment on a little house. I'll hire on elsewhere. I can't ask Angus to pay me a wage when I owe him money for those taxes. I'll see if he can wait a while for me to pay him back. You can live here for a year or two then we'll find a house in a small town somewhere. We just can't afford a ranch of our own."

"I don't want to live in a town," Jenny protested, but Matt cut her off.

"We'll see how much I can get for my land and add whatever I can save to it. Maybe then we can buy a small ranch."

There was a commotion at the front door followed by the hammer of little feet running down the hallway.

A second later, he burst into the kitchen. "Angus and Mora want to talk to you."

"Her name is Moira," Jenny said.

"That's what I said, Mora." Jesse ran back out of the room.

Matt stood and stared down at Jenny. "Don't move," he said, drinking his fill of her. Her hair was loose and it curled in long waves across her shoulders, echoing all the curves of her body. Matt was looking forward to spending the rest of his life learning all her nooks and crannies.

Moira and Angus sat in the living room. Matt greeted them both with a bear hug for Angus and a gentle hug for the pretty woman with him.

They suited each other, felt right together.

Jesse lay on the floor turning the pages of a new book that Angus must have brought home for him.

"Sit down," Angus said. "I have a proposition for both of you."

He was speaking to Matt and Jenny, but Jesse piped up. "Me, too?"

"Of course for you, too," Angus answered. "I wouldn't leave you out."

Angus took Moira's hand in his and smiled down at her. "Matt, we want to make you an offer on your land."

"What?" Matt felt his mouth fall open, but he couldn't seem to comprehend what Angus had just said.

"I'm serious, Matt." Angus named a figure that curled Matt's toes.

"It can't possibly be worth that much."

"Matt, because of everything that went wrong in that house, you haven't been able to see it clearly, but the land is real pretty."

"Really?"

"Yes," Moira answered. "It's beautiful."

"Still Creek runs through it," Angus said, as though that explained everything.

"But how can you possibly move all your cattle there? The property isn't large enough."

"Well," Angus said, "I'd like to sell the cattle to you when you buy this ranch."

Matt left his armchair. "What?" He paced to the window. "You're joking, right?"

Angus was dead serious. "What I'll pay for your land will make a solid down payment for this place. You'll have no trouble getting a mortgage for the rest."

"You're *not* joking?" Matt turned to look at Jenny. A wide grin graced her face. Her eyes glistened suspiciously.

Matt couldn't believe it yet. "You're a rancher, Angus. How can you give this up?"

"I lost my drive after I lost Kyle. The ranch just doesn't mean as much to me anymore. I thought I could get that back by marrying Jenny and having more children, but that was unreasonable."

He glanced at Moira and smiled. "We want to raise bison. Your land is perfect. We want it. We want to sell you this ranch. I'd say that makes life pretty well perfect for all of us."

Matt noticed Jesse smiling, but looking bewildered. He picked him up. "Jesse, remember your mom and I said we would have to move away from this ranch?"

Jesse bobbed his head.

"We won't have to anymore," Matt said. Lord, he felt his own eyes get damp. "We're going to live here forever."

Jesse fought to get out of Matt's arms then started to

dance in the middle of the room. To Matt, he was goofy and wound up and perfect.

Jenny joined Matt and wrapped her arms around his waist. She rested her head on his chest and he gripped her hard.

How had all of this come out of that awful house he grew up in and his sorrow-filled childhood?

Angus stood and laid one hand on Matt's shoulder. He cleared his throat.

"There is a catch."

Matt should have known it couldn't possibly be as perfect as it sounded. Then he saw the twinkle in Angus's eyes.

"We want to tear down that old house and build our own."

Okay, Angus's already perfect offer just became even more so. Matt was no longer angry about the things that had happened in that house. Now he felt deep sorrow.

Getting rid of the house would close the last chapter of his childhood.

He shook Angus's hand. "It's a deal."

Out of the blue, Angus looked unsure of himself. "There is one more stipulation."

"What?" Matt asked warily.

"I would like to be honorary grandfather to your children."

"Cripes, Angus, of course!" Then Matt was hugging both Angus and Jenny, his two best friends in the world.

Jenny pulled out of his arms and knelt in front of their son.

"Would you like Angus to be your grandfather?"

"Yeah!" Jesse pointed to Moira. "Is she my grandma?"

Jenny turned to the older woman. "I don't know. Give me time."

Moira said, "I understand."

"Jesse," Jenny said. "There's even more good news. Matt is your daddy."

"You mean like Angus was gonna be my daddy after you married him? Now Matt is instead?"

"Matt isn't going to be your father because I'm marrying him. Matt *is* your daddy, your really, truly, forever-after father."

Jesse started dancing again.

Matt wasn't sure how much happiness one body could hold, but he did know that the more he held, the bigger he felt. He was learning that there was no limit to how much a man could grow, or how much he could become.

EPILOGUE

ROSE SQUIRMED in Matt's arms as he stepped out of the church and into the bright frosty sunshine. He sheltered her with his chest, provided shade with his shoulder and she settled.

Jenny and Jesse walked on either side of him, just as they had when Matt and Jenny had gotten married last June. They'd conceived little Rose soon after.

Rose's godparents, Angus and Moira, followed.

Reverend Wright had performed a beautiful baptism ceremony.

Many of Ordinary's citizens who were now his friends gathered around.

Angel Donovan stood in the crowd and smiled at Matt. They'd gotten to know each other over the holidays. Missy and Angel had joined Matt, Jenny and Jesse for Christmas dinner, along with Angus and Moira, just like a real family. Angel hadn't known who her real father was, as Missy had always refused to tell her. Angel was having trouble dealing with Missy's omission, but she was working on it. One thing she had told Matt was that she liked having a brother.

Like her mother, Angel was a knockout. Matt saw the way some of the younger men were looking at his sister, and scowled at a couple of them, feeling very much like a big brother. But he knew that Angel was a grown woman who would make her own choices.

Their footsteps crunched on dry late-February snow.

Hank and Amy wanted pictures. Matt stopped on the steps, pulled his wife against his side and kissed her, long enough and passionately enough that the crowd hooted.

When he finished, Jenny's cheeks were rosy. She smiled and picked up Jesse.

Angus and Moira stood behind them.

Camera shutters clicked.

Matt thought back to the first time he'd ever made love to Jenny. He remembered sitting in his truck and staring at his parents' house. Lightning had lit the place up like a photographic flash, catching a freeze-frame image of a sad history.

That image had defined his life for too many years.

No longer.

The house was gone now. Angus and Moira had built a pretty Victorian home in its place and Matt and Jenny and Jesse visited often.

That clearing held good memories now.

Hank said, "One more," and took a last shot.

Matt knew what these images would show—a happy couple with their two children, in front of another happy couple, the honorary grandparents, all of them surrounded by brilliant white snow.

While the photos were being shot, Jesse pointed to each member of his family and named them. In the second-to-last photo, he pointed to Rose and said, "That's my sister, Rose."

In the last photo that Hank shot, Jesse pointed to Matt and said, "That's my dad."

Matt ruffled Jesse's hair and then kissed Rose's tiny pink forehead.

Yeah. Matt was a dad. And he was here to stay.

* * * * *

HARLEQUIN® *Super Romance*®

COMING NEXT MONTH

Available September 14, 2010

LARGER-PRINT BOOKS!
GET 2 FREE LARGER-PRINT NOVELS PLUS
2 FREE GIFTS!

HARLEQUIN®

Super Romance

Exciting, emotional, unexpected!

YES! Please send me 2 FREE LARGER-PRINT Harlequin® Superromance® novels and my 2 FREE gifts (gifts are worth about $10). After receiving them, if I don't wish to receive any more books, I can return the shipping statement marked "cancel." If I don't cancel, I will receive 6 brand-new novels every month and be billed just $5.44 per book in the U.S. or $5.99 per book in Canada. That's a saving of at least 13% off the cover price! It's quite a bargain! Shipping and handling is just 50¢ per book.* I understand that accepting the 2 free books and gifts places me under no obligation to buy anything. I can always return a shipment and cancel at any time. Even if I never buy another book from Harlequin, the two free books and gifts are mine to keep forever.

139/339 HDN E5PS

Name _____ (PLEASE PRINT) _____

Address _____ Apt. # _____

City _____ State/Prov. _____ Zip/Postal Code _____

Signature (if under 18, a parent or guardian must sign) _____

Mail to the **Harlequin Reader Service:**
IN U.S.A.: P.O. Box 1867, Buffalo, NY 14240-1867
IN CANADA: P.O. Box 609, Fort Erie, Ontario L2A 5X3

Not valid for current subscribers to Harlequin Superromance Larger-Print books.

**Are you a current subscriber to Harlequin Superromance books
and want to receive the larger-print edition?
Call 1-800-873-8635 today!**

* Terms and prices subject to change without notice. Prices do not include applicable taxes. N.Y. residents add applicable sales tax. Canadian residents will be charged applicable provincial taxes and GST. Offer not valid in Quebec. This offer is limited to one order per household. All orders subject to approval. Credit or debit balances in a customer's account(s) may be offset by any other outstanding balance owed by or to the customer. Please allow 4 to 6 weeks for delivery. Offer available while quantities last.

Your Privacy: Harlequin Books is committed to protecting your privacy. Our Privacy Policy is available online at www.eHarlequin.com or upon request from the Reader Service. From time to time we make our lists of customers available to reputable third parties who may have a product or service of interest to you. If you would prefer we not share your name and address, please check here. ☐

Help us get it right—We strive for accurate, respectful and relevant communications. To clarify or modify your communication preferences, visit us at www.ReaderService.com/consumerchoice.

HSRLP10R

HARLEQUIN®

A Romance

FOR EVERY MOOD™

Spotlight on

── Heart & Home ──

Heartwarming romances
where love can happen
right when you least expect it.

See the next page to enjoy a sneak peek
from Harlequin Superromance®,
a Heart and Home series.

Enjoy a sneak peek at fan favorite Molly O'Keefe's
Harlequin Superromance miniseries,
THE NOTORIOUS O'NEILLS, *with*
TYLER O'NEILL'S REDEMPTION,
available September 2010
only from Harlequin Superromance.

Police chief Juliette Tremblant recognized the shape of the man strolling down the street—in as calm and leisurely fashion as if it were the middle of the day rather than midnight. She slowed her car, convinced her eyes were playing tricks on her. It had been a long time since Tyler O'Neill had been seen in this town.

As she pulled to a stop at the curb, he turned toward her, and her heart about stopped.

"What the hell are you doing here, Tyler?"

"Well, if it isn't Juliette Tremblant." He made his way over to her, then leaned down so he could look her in the eye. He was close enough to touch.

Juliette was not, repeat, *not* going to touch Tyler O'Neill. Not with her fingers. Not with a ten-foot pole. There would be no touching. Which was too bad, since it was the only way she was ever going to convince herself the man standing in front of her—as rumpled and heart-stoppingly handsome now as he'd been at sixteen—was real.

And not a figment of all her furious revenge dreams.

"What are you doing back in Bonne Terre?" she asked.

"The manor is sitting empty," Tyler said and shrugged, as though his arriving out of the blue after ten years was casual. "Seems like someone should be watching over the family home."

"You?" She laughed at the very notion of him being here for any unselfish reason. "Please."

He stared at her for a second, then smiled. Her heart fluttered against her chest—a small mechanical bird powered by that smile.

"You're right." But that cryptic comment was all he offered.

Juliette bit her lip against the other questions.

Why did you go?

Why didn't you write? Call?

What did I do?

But what would be the point? Ten years of silence were all the answer she really needed.

She had sworn off feeling anything for this man long ago. Yet one look at him and all the old hurt and rage resurfaced as though they'd been waiting for the chance. That made her mad.

She put the car in gear, determined not to waste another minute thinking about Tyler O'Neill. "Have a good night, Tyler," she said, liking all the cool "go screw yourself" she managed to fit into those words.

It seems Juliette has an old score to settle with Tyler.
Pick up TYLER O'NEILL'S REDEMPTION
to see how he makes it up to her.
Available September 2010,
only from Harlequin Superromance.

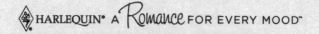

Love Inspired®

Fan Favorite
Janet Tronstad

brings readers a heartwarming story
of love and hope with

Dr. Right

Treasure Creek, Alaska, has only one pediatrician:
the very handsome, very eligible Dr. Alex Haven.
With his contract coming to an end, he plans
to return home to Los Angeles. But Nurse
Maryann Jenner is determined to keep Alex
in Alaska, and when a little boy's life—and
Maryann's hope—is jeopardized, Alex may
find a reason to stay forever.

ALASKAN *Bride* RUSH

Available September wherever books are sold.

Steeple
Hill®

LI87620

HARLEQUIN *Super Romance*

Watch out
for a whole new look for
Harlequin Superromance,
coming soon!

*The same great stories you love
with a brand-new look!*

Unexpected, exciting
and emotional stories
about life and falling in love.

Coming soon!